PRAISE FOR RELATIVELY PAINLESS

"My only complaint is that I wanted more, which is a good complaint to have. It made me laugh and cry and then laugh again and then pee and then cry. Lots of fluids lost. But in a good way. A book to make you appreciate the tragically funny and beautiful horror of family."

— Jenny Lawson

PRAISE FOR THE AUTHOR

"Dylan Brody is funny in ways that don't remind me of anyone."

– David Sedaris

"His writing is brilliant."

– Robin Williams

"... the twists of his psyche are cathartic for him and thrilling for an audience."

– Richard Lewis

Also By Dylan Brody

BOOKS

——

Laughs Last
A Manifesto of Radical Optimism
The Modern Depression Guidebook
The Warm Hello
A Tale of a Hero and the Song of Her Sword
Heroes Fall (novella)

CDs

——

Writ Large
Chronological Disorder
A Twist of the Wit
True Enough
Brevity
Road Tested (coming soon)

RELATIVELY PAINLESS

DYLAN BRODY

atmosphere press

CONTENTS

WEIGHT

Paul and Ellen said the last goodbyes at the Mathesons' front door as the kids crunched down the walkway through the snow. Each step broke through the thin frozen layer. The soft powder underneath compressed with a gentle squeak.

Daniel pushed his hands into his pockets and kept his eyes on the slight depression that marked the pathway. Lindsay said, "It's not gonna be any warmer in the car."

Daniel said, "Yeah." Then, after another moment, "They won't be long."

Lindsay made a snorty noise that Daniel recognized as one she had learned from their father.

Behind them, Ellen laughed louder than could possibly have been warranted by anything short of a Richard Pryor punch line. She would have said Jack Benny. Daniel made the same snorting noise he had just heard his big sister make.

Lindsay chuckled at the sound, not having recognized it when it came from her own sinuses but knowing it instantly when it came from Daniel's. She worked the latch with cold fingers and then pulled the car door open. Daniel climbed in, hands-and-kneesing across the pleather bench to the driver's side. Lindsay took her own seat behind the empty front passenger's seat. She pulled the door closed with a crunchy slam and they sat together in the cold car, waiting.

Daniel blew into his cold hands.

Lindsay fastened her seatbelt with a chilly click.

Beyond the glass, at the far end of the snow-frozen walkway, their parents had not yet turned away from the Mathesons.

"I made Gary laugh twice at dinner."

Lindsay said, "Gary's a pig."

Daniel shrugged. "I like him."

"You like anyone who laughs at your stupid jokes."

"Not just the stupid ones."

"What?"

"Why is he a pig?"

Lindsay shook her head in a way that suggested she thought Daniel was an idiot. "He just sits there chatting with Mom and Dad while Louise brings out dinner, serves everyone, then after dinner, she's up and clearing the table and he just sits there with Mom and Dad talking about what kind of scotch he likes. And then, and then she picks up his ashtray to empty like she's some kind of a maid and—did you see?—he slaps her on the ass? And you don't see why I think he's a pig?"

"I don't think she minded it."

"Which?"

"Any of it. I think she was having a good time."

Lindsay said nothing then. Daniel knew she was mad at him now, but he didn't understand why other than that he had disagreed with her.

Paul and Ellen had gotten halfway down the path now,

but they stopped and turned back to shout a last remark at their hosts. The Mathesons laughed and waved them off. They went in and shut the door, closing the light inside. Paul held Ellen's elbow to steady her as they made their way through the crunching, squeaking snow. He didn't seem much steadier than she did.

He circled the car to get in the driver's seat as Ellen slid in on the passenger's side in front of Lindsay. She pulled the door closed and pulled the shoulder harness across her body, snapping it into its latch. Paul started up the car, turned on the heat and left it in neutral, gently pressing and releasing the gas pedal. He waited a full two minutes like that before the temperature gauge started to show a response. Then he put the transmission into drive and pulled away from the curb.

He drove in silence until the car slipped onto Route Twenty-Nine. After another thirty seconds or so, Ellen said, "Gary said I look terrific."

Paul said, "He's gotten really heavy."

"Louise is in great shape."

"She runs. I see her on campus."

"Running, you mean?"

"Yeah."

"He really has gotten soft." Then after a moment's pause, "Still, it was nice to hear that I look terrific."

"I tell you that."

"Yeah, yeah."

"I tell you that all the time."

"You have to say that. You're my husband."

"I have to say that?"

"Yes."

"I had no idea. I was just saying it when I noticed how

terrific you look."

"Very funny."

Lindsay sighed.

Daniel said, "I like Gary."

Ellen said, "That's because he laughs at your jokes."

Paul said, "You were funny tonight."

Ellen said, "Paul, don't encourage."

The car fishtailed on the ice and in a tense moment Paul focused on the road, turned into the skid and regained control of the car on the dark, empty highway.

Ellen said, "He was really flirting with me, I think."

Lindsay murmured, "Jesus," very quietly, her derision a small performance for Daniel. He did not know why she seemed so angry.

Paul said, "Who could blame him? You look terrific."

Ellen punched Paul in the arm as he drove, not hard, not angrily. "You think it bothers him that you haven't— you know . . ."

"Gotten soft?"

"Yeah."

Lindsay said, now loudly enough to be heard from the front seat, "Maybe they don't obsess about the weight of everyone they encounter."

Paul said, "I don't think we obsess."

Lindsay made the snorting noise.

Ellen said, "Don't do that, Linds."

Paul said something then, but the rocking of the car and the slow-spreading warmth had begun to take its toll on Daniel. His forehead rested against the cool glass of the window for a moment and then he changed his position so he could curl up on the wide bench. His head rested on his sister's lap and she allowed it.

She ran her fingers through his hair and then circled a fingertip gently against his temple.

The conversation from the front seat reached him as sleep muffled murmurs, but the words did not really matter. He had heard them many times before, the discussion as familiar as the smell of laundry detergent, as predictable as the Thursday night television lineup.

He did not fully understand what it meant to obsess. He did not know whether it was something his parents did or not. He knew that weight was what they talked about after visiting people. He knew that they spoke about Lindsay's weight in a near whisper when she was not in the room.

He fought his way back to the surface for a moment, struggled to remain conscious and said to his sister, "I think you look terrific, Lindsay."

Lindsay said, "You don't have to say that, Dan."

"I know."

"If you're not going to sleep, I'm kicking you off my lap."

So, he stopped talking then and allowed the darkness to rise about him like water. In his dreams he was buoyant, floating. Paul and Ellen compared their own appearance to that of their erstwhile hosts as the car rolled up over the seasonal frost heaves, the gentle inclines. At the peak of each rise, the momentum of the vehicle nearly lifted it from the pavement. In those moments, head resting on his older sister's sharp, dancer's thigh, the delightful sensation reminded Daniel of Gary's effortless, friendly laugh as he experienced just a taste of weightlessness.

VENT

They huddled over the vent, the Grunman children. Not for heat today but to listen. They crouched on the floor of their parents' bedroom, directly above the kitchen, and tried to make out the words. The tenor, clear, terrified them. Much of what was said below came muffled, distorted by the hidden ducts. They strained against the echo and ring to find sense in the syllables.

Their mother's anger rose to peak volume and then tensed to a feline growl. Then their father, his rage a clenched threat, gripped an apology between feral jaws. They had never heard this before, this fury in their home. So, they huddled. They listened.

Daniel, the younger of the two, said, "Do you think—?"

Lindsay cut him off with a look. Nine years old, she had already learned her mother's warning glare.

Daniel's eyes widened at her, an expression of urgency. She put a finger to her lips telling him that if he absolutely must speak, he should do it softly. He whispered. "Do you think we're not going?"

They were both already dressed for the outdoors, for the cool spring day, for a promised visit to the carnival that

8

had set up in the wide parking lot of the A&P in Saratoga Springs. They had started with the casual mention of the flyer they'd seen on the bulletin board at school, then escalated to carefully timed imaginings of what it would be like as off-handed dinner conversation. They had slowly, deliberately led their parents to come to their own decision that it would be a fun activity for the whole family. Perhaps over the weekend. Yes. Maybe on Sunday, late morning when it would be less crowded; so many families would be at church, they might nearly have the whole place to themselves.

Daniel mostly loved the rides. He loved the feeling of motion and danger although he never screamed and shrieked like the other children. He would feel a grin coming on as he reached the front of the queue and it would stay with him as he walked the shaky plank to the roller coaster car or the Ferris wheel carriage, to the Tilt-a-Whirl seat like a vinyl-booth diner bench in a tin bubble. He would nod at the young grown-ups whose job it was to lower the safety bars in front of him and then, as the ride started, he would shift into a mindset of analytical intellect. *There's no actual danger,* he would remind himself in that sub-lingual way of inner soothing. *The place would be shut down if people got hurt.* He would sit as others screamed around him, feeling the shift and pull of the great centrifuge, the rise and peak of the squeaking swing cage, the time bomb ticking of the upward incline and the weightless drop of that first plummeting coast. He turned inward to find the muscle groups reacting to the unexpected banking left, the sudden lurching halt, the pressing shift of momentum. He loved each of these as though every moment was its own micro-adventure and he prided himself on his ability to enjoy the sensation without the screeching panic that took so many people as they rose and fell, as they rotated and revolved. As he stepped away from each, again the grin would take him, the sheer joy of it all, the anticipation of the next thrill that he might examine from just enough of a psychic distance that it could not touch him.

Lindsay had very little interest in most of the rides, save the Tilt-a-Whirl which she said reminded her of what she always wanted dancing to feel like. She loved the mazes and the fun houses. From the scare-at-every-turn spooky palace to the labyrinth of mirrors, if she could hand someone tickets to walk through a doorway, she would pay the price to enter the warren. Once, at the small amusement park at Kadyross Lake, Daniel had stood outside watching her navigate the house of glass. As others about her, kids and adults alike, took delight in bumping up against transparent dead ends and struggling with the low-level anxiety of claustrophobic disorientation, Lindsay walked the maze, head down, pace so steady she might as well have been coming home from school, text books under her arm. Once she started down a wrong corridor, stopped before reaching the end, retraced her steps and resumed her walk to the exit.

"You didn't look like you were having any fun at all," he said to her.

"It's not as hard as it looks," she said. Then, after a brief pause, "I think most people pretend it's hard, so they feel like it's worth the price." She headed immediately for a fun house with the slanty floors and the glow-in-the-dark perspective illusions and he tagged after his older sister.

"The rides too. People scream like it's scary."

She shrugged then. "I like the mazes. Puzzles. You know?"

He didn't but he said, "Uh-huh," anyway.

Listening to the fight shouting and rumbling up through the branching, bending ductwork, Daniel and Lindsay could sense one another's fear.

Their parents argued from time to time but that took the form of disagreements, usually about what the kids should or shouldn't eat at what time of day or whether they were flush enough as a family to go to a movie opening weekend or if they would have to wait until the next paycheck came in. Whoever lost such a dispute would put up his or her hands in defeat and say, "Okay, okay." And then after a moment, "But I get points." The points supposedly could be cashed in on a future disagreement. They never were. Sometimes if Dad got his feelings hurt, he might take cruel verbal jabs at his wife over dinner, caustic jokes with an antiseptic sting. When Mom carried resentment over something, she took on an overly cheerful tone and chattered on about innocuous inanities as though she might paint over her displeasure in bright hues of desperate yellow. The very worst of arguments consisted of a few curt words and then an hour of silence underscored by the measured drone of National Public Radio's *All Things Considered*.

Today, though, the conflict felt violent to the children, listening, eyes wide as though that might help them hear the details hidden in the strident cadence and tone of dark, tunnel-muffled confrontation.

Then silence broke up through the shaft. Lindsay and Daniel looked at one another's eyes, their senses reaching out toward the staircase. They both knew in the way that young siblings know a thing without thinking it odd to share a thought that if they heard footsteps on the stairs they would have to pretend to be playing, not listening.

No footsteps came. The fourth step did not creak under the weight of an adult.

The silence lasted what seemed a very long time. Then loud footsteps crossed the kitchen floor and a door slammed.

Lindsay moved to the window and looked out. She said, "It's Dad. He didn't take the car."

"Going for a walk."

"Yeah. Hands in his pockets. He looks pissed."

They crept down the stairs together. They went one at a time over the fourth step so it would not creak, and they sat on those bottom steps below the turn that allowed them to see their mother's back. She stood at the sink, washing dishes with a vigor breakfast dishes could not possibly require.

Lindsay said, "You should say something to her."

"Why me?"

"'Cause you're the funny one. Make her laugh or . . . comfort her or . . . Cheer her up." He hesitated, so she added, "Maybe if you get her talking, we can find out what's going on."

Daniel nodded. He stepped up to the kitchen door and breathed, hoping his mother would hear him. A shift in her breathing suggested she had, a sharp sniff that ended a tense, muttering snuffle. He said, "Hey, Mom . . .?"

She said, "What?" but her focus stayed on the scrubbing of a clean cereal bowl.

He wanted to say, "What were you guys fighting

about?" He wanted to say, "Lindsay and I don't know what's going on and we're scared." He wanted to say, "Are you okay?" He did not say any of those things, though he paused as each of them ran through his head. He thought to turn toward happier thoughts. He said, "Do you think there'll be a Tilt-a-Whirl at the carnival?"

His mother turned off the water and set the bowl aside. She stood for a half a second, maybe a full second, holding the edge of the sink and then she turned to face him. He thought for sure this was what a person's eyes looked like from the outside when they saw red. Her words came out crisp and quiet and terrifyingly controlled. "You have got to be the most insensitive, self-involved human being I have ever known."

He heard her rage, her disappointment. He heard her words. "No. For Lindsay. It's the only ride she likes." He did not know why that was what he had asked rather than whatever it was that his mother would have preferred he ask. He was almost certain that none of the questions he really wanted to ask was what she would have wanted anyway.

"Uh-huh." She continued to study him with those blood-stained eyes, lip quivering between a sneer and a snarl until he backed away, imagining apologies he dared not voice.

His calves touched the bottom stair and he sat on the cool hardwood of the tread, realizing that his sister had vanished.

His mother returned to the kitchen, not to the sink where he could see her but to the table out of his frame of vision. He pictured her sitting there, furious, wondering how she had raised such an unfeeling monster. He considered finding Lindsay and yelling at her for making him do that, but he knew it had not been her fault. He had said the wrong thing. He had made it all worse. He wanted someone to comfort him, to cheer him up. He could not imagine who might do that, or how.

An hour later their father returned. There was some conversation in the kitchen that the kids could not hear. They did not try. Then Dad yelled, "You guys about ready to go?"

"We're still going?"

"That was the plan, wasn't it?"

They climbed into the car, grown-ups in front, kids in back. Dad drove, making the occasional joke. Mom read road signs aloud, turned the radio on for a bit and then turned it off to talk about what she'd just heard.

Behind them, seen only by Daniel, Lindsay looked down at her knees, eyebrows pushed toward one another as though a complex puzzle troubled her deeply. Daniel watched her for a bit. Then he closed his eyes and listened to his mother's soothing chatter. He felt his weight move with the shifts in momentum as the Grunmans hurtled toward the flash and chaos of the Dreamland Carnival, toward the rickety gear contraptions maintained by gap toothed mechanics and operated by acne scarred adolescents, toward the waiting rides where Daniel would wheel and fly and fall and he would feel safe.

SILENT

Part of the fun of the nights that Paul took Daniel to the movies on campus was that the boy so loved comedy. Lindsay never showed much interest unless it was a musical that was likely to have dance sequences, but Daniel was different. Any chance he got to experience the grown-up world he would take. He absorbed the world around him with a seriousness that surprised people who didn't live in the same house with him. His questions went beyond the ordinary curiosity of a child. He came to them from a place of insight and sought increased depth.

The group of students who decided what movies would come up from New York in their big hexagonal boxes for projection in the student center on Friday nights couldn't always be trusted to have the best taste, but comedies and science fiction always drew Daniel's interest. Daniel would go through the schedule and highlight the ones he wanted to go to. If he didn't have something else—and he almost never did—Paul took him to the films, even the ones the boy was unlikely to fully understand.

On the drives back afterward, Daniel would sit in the

front seat with him. He would fold his legs up under him so that he could rest his forehead against the window and watch the world go by and then he would turn to say something that blew Paul's mind, that small boy with the quick wit and the wonderful questions.

After 2001—A SPACE ODYSSEY, Daniel had been silent all the way to the car. He had gotten in without a word and knelt on the passenger's seat lost in thought. Paul had the sense that he was running the whole film over in his mind a frame at a time, trying to make sense of it all. About ten minutes from home, he finally spoke. "I think that movie is only pretending to be about space. I think it's actually about time."

They had explored that thought together for the remainder of the drive. Daniel's level of intellect constantly startled Paul, whether it expressed as insight or as humor. Ellen often referred to the boy as being seven going on forty and Paul wondered if that somehow registered as pressure for the child, but he understood what she meant.

Once, a visiting professor had stayed in the guest room. He'd gotten up early and had breakfast with the kids before they went off to school. When Paul got out of the shower, dressed and came downstairs, he found the man sipping coffee, bemused. He asked if the professor was okay and he'd said, "I'm fine. I just spent fifteen minutes exchanging one-liners with a six-year-old."

"Yeah. He's something, isn't he? I think he knows about five thousand jokes."

Professor Dimitri shook his head slowly. "Maybe but . . . I think he was making some of them up on the spot."

"He might've been. Sometimes it's hard to tell."

Now, as they sat together waiting for the movie to

start, Paul was as excited as his son, even if he was better able to contain his enthusiasm. He remembered Daniel's response to the Marx Brothers. He remembered Daniel's joy at his discovery of Charlie Chaplin. Tonight would be one of those nights. Daniel was about to get his first taste of Buster Keaton and through his son, Paul would get to see the stone-faced stuntman anew again.

Daniel bounced in his seat. He swung his legs. He practically vibrated with anticipation.

"Settle down, Dee,"

Daniel said, "Okay." Then, "Sorry." Then, after a minute, "Butch Brown?"

"Buster Keaton."

"Right."

Then the lights went down, and the movie began.

Many of the college students, he realized, were probably seeing these gags for the first time just like his son. While they laughed and cheered, Daniel watched, eyes wide. Whenever Paul glanced over, he found Daniel grinning up into the flicker.

Daniel stared as Buster's car got caught on the tracks. He tried to restart it. He tried to push it. The train approached. He tried to move the car and at the last possible moment gave up and ran away as the train blasted through on the next track over, missing the car entirely. The room burst into laughter and Buster, relieved, turned to walk back toward the car. A train came from the other direction and destroyed the vehicle. Buster stumbled back a step, tripped, fell on his ass, rolled back into a reverse somersault and came back to his feet dusting himself off, casting a sad look of betrayal toward the receding train. Daniel barked a sharp, "Hah!"

It wasn't a true laugh. It was a startled, excited acknowledgement of a perfectly constructed sight gag. Paul glanced over, and Daniel nodded his approval of the film, or of the joke, or of the acrobatic skill. Paul nodded back, agreeing with whatever it was that Daniel approved of.

Paul was not old enough to have seen first run Keaton, of course. But he had discovered the silents at an art house in San Francisco during the three years he and Ellen had lived there in the late fifties. He had fallen in love with them then, finding them funny and engrossing in a way none of the films of his childhood had been. He wondered now if he'd laughed or just barked in intellectual approval.

He remembered going to the Purple Onion and seeing the great comedians of the time working out their material. He still had a reel-to-reel tape he'd made of that evening, but it was not the performances he remembered most clearly. It was seeing the comics sitting at a table near the back of the room, watching one another perform as they prepared for or came down from their own sets. It was fascinating to see the way professionals watched comedy. They didn't laugh, not often at least. Mostly they sat in appreciative silence as if it was a ballet they witnessed or a Pinter play. The better the joke, the more they nodded. When someone at that table laughed, it was often at a joke that the rest of the audience failed to reward, a signal of approval in the face of dissenting public opinion.

Was it genetic? Where did that kind of observational removal originate?

After the film, while all the students filed out, Daniel kept his seat, looking up at the white screen as if the movie might start again at any moment. Paul sat beside him, wondering what he was thinking. He found himself trying to imagine what the experience had been for the boy. His boy.

When the theater was empty except for a kid whose work study arrangement had him sweeping out the dropped popcorn and collecting the discarded soda cups, Paul said, "You about ready?"

"Yeah." But then there was a long pause before Daniel stood up and let the spring-loaded seat fold itself back up flat against the seatback.

Paul lit a cigarette as they walked up the aisle. Daniel remained very quiet. His eyes narrowed from time to time as though he was trying to see something in the far distance, though Paul had known him long enough to know that he was just thinking, sorting through complex ideas.

They got into the car. Daniel did a bit of schtick as he opened the door, smacking it with his hand and snapping his head back to make it seem he had hit himself in the nose. He didn't do it with full commitment; it was just a small experiment in physical comedy, but he looked up at Paul to see if he'd gotten a laugh. Paul realized he knew something about how comedy works. "It'll never work if you check for the reaction afterward."

Daniel nodded. He said, "Huh."

He climbed into his kneeling position in the front, the seat he only got when the two of them were alone in the car. If Ellen was with them, she got the front seat, naturally, and when both kids were in the car, they both sat in the back to avoid arguments and resentments.

Paul drove and pretended not to notice Daniel picking

his nose absently over to his right. Eventually Daniel spoke confidently. "I think I could do that."

"Yeah?"

"Yeah. I mean—I think I'd have to learn some stuff so I wouldn't get hurt, but I think I could do almost all of those bits.'

Paul nodded. He imparted a little bit of father's wisdom. "The mark of the great artists is that they make it look effortless."

Daniel went silent for a long, long while.

Paul fought the urge to ask him what he was thinking. He wanted to hear the details of what went on in that kid's head. He wanted to break down the machinations, deconstruct the process of learning and thinking but he knew that he would not get the answers he sought. He would get some cryptic statement or some simple observation, droplets that hinted at unseen waterfalls, dust motes hanging bright in a shaft of light that implied a sun just out of frame.

"You enjoyed it."

"Yeah! A lot." Then, after a moment, "Next week is The Skinny Man."

"*The Thin Man.*"

"I know," Daniel lied. "I like to call it The Skinny Man."

Paul said, "No you don't. You got it wrong." They sat in silence for a moment. "Yeah?"

Daniel nodded. "Yeah."

They rode in silence for a moment. "Do you understand why the truth is important, Daniel?"

"Yeah," Daniel lied. He waited a moment, just to find out if there would be clarification, but he couldn't ask now that he'd claimed to understand, and Paul was aware of all of it. He wanted to call the boy on it again, but it seemed to him that it might be good for the kid to know that he could have secrets, that people would not always be able to see through the lies, that it would be up to him alone to maintain integrity. "Is that a comedy?"

"It is. It's a mystery and a comedy. It might be a little bit complicated for you."

"Okay." Then, "But we can go anyway. Right?"

"I'll check my calendar."

They rode together, Paul watching the road, Daniel watching the passing landscape. After what seemed to Paul like much too long to be the same conversation, Daniel said, "You'll check your calendar."

"I will."

"Okay."

They rode in silence. Paul did not know what Daniel was thinking about. Paul thought about his own father, about moments decades earlier in a much larger car with a man who always seemed on the verge of rage. He wondered if he was ruining his son.

He knew that he was the only father in town who did not play catch with his kid, who did not coach a sport. He didn't know anything about hunting or fishing.

He worried that Daniel might not be having any of the fun that childhood was supposed to provide. The boy seemed so serious. Even about comedy he seemed serious.

The lying looked like it could become a problem, too. He wasn't sure what that was about. He would keep an eye on it, he decided. Maybe the boy was just testing boundaries, finding out where he ended and other people began.

He glanced over and found that Daniel had dozed off,

face pressed against the cool glass of his window. He opened the window on his side of the car, just a crack, and lit a cigarette.

He pulled smoke into his lungs and wondered if he should buy a sixteen-millimeter movie camera for Daniel to experiment with. He imagined the boy running around doing stunts for laughs, pratfalls and sight gags. He chuckled in the silence.

Daniel stirred in his sleep and muttered, "What's funny."

Paul said, "You can sleep, buddy. Nothing's funny."

Daniel said, "Boy, I hope that's not true."

He was already asleep again, so he did not see Paul, driving through the silent night, nod his approval rather than laughing.

CATCH

Daniel stood at the bar outside the showroom at Catch A Rising Star. He wrapped his hands around his coffee cup for warmth. He always felt as though he was freezing to death before he performed. It started the moment he left his dorm room to get the train into the city. It lasted until the moment he walked on stage. To make matters worse, he always got to whatever club he was playing before the start of the show regardless of what time his spot was. He took it all very seriously and although they only told him the particular time that he would be performing, he treated it like a proper show, assuming his call time was half an hour before curtain.

The bartender, whose name he had never bothered to learn, refilled his cup from a coffee pot. Not many people at the club drank coffee. He was the only person in the club who was not old enough to drink alcohol.

The crowd in the bar started to shift toward the show room doors. He was never certain how they knew when it was time, but it happened every night. They hung out drinking and chatting and then the shift would happen. They would begin to gravitate toward the show room as though drawn by an alluring aroma. That wasn't it, though. No night club he had entered to date had anything that could be described as an alluring aroma.

Kevin, the house manager shouted, "Ladies and gentlemen! The house is open. You may bring your drinks with you, but they will not count toward your two-item minimum! We'll try to get you all seated as quickly as possible and waitresses will be around to start taking orders. We should be able to get this cavalcade of talent . . . and other performers, started right at eight o'clock for you."

Daniel had heard the speech twenty or thirty times now. The people always laughed at the little jokes, already primed to respond, anticipating the hilarity they imagined was to come. He pulled his little spiral-bound notebook from his back pocket and jotted down a thought about the way people approach the evening with hope that he might ask them to rekindle upon his arrival on the stage. He didn't quite feel it was something he could do yet but there was something there to play with.

As the audience moved into the showroom, slowly emptying the bar, the front door opened and his older sister, Lindsay came in mouthing, "I'm so sorry," at him as she crossed the bar to hug him, their parents just behind her apparently engaged in a dispute with the pneumatic door closer.

Daniel whispered into her ear, "What the hell?"

"I told them. They wouldn't listen."

"Jesus."

"Right?"

Paul and Ellen, having concluded whatever the hell they had been up to at the door, approached him. Paul opened his arms for a hug and Daniel obliged. His mother moved in for her hug next, then she stepped back and looked at her son. She said, "When did you get so tall?"

"What the hell, guys?"

Paul said, "You invited us."

"Yes. Yes, I did. And I told you that I'll probably be going up around twelve-thirty or one."

Ellen said, "You said it was all just one show and it starts at 8:oo."

"Yeah, but I also said you didn't need to get here until around eleven-thirty or twelve when the late emcee takes over."

Paul said, "We almost never go out that late. You know that."

Daniel blinked slowly.

Ellen said, "Oooh! They're going in. I'm going to try to get us seats in the back. I don't want them to make fun of me." She moved for the door and Paul followed, giving his son an encouraging smile and throwing a gesture that was intended to be, "We'll see you in there," but actually seemed to imply, "You and I will use a vertical Spirograph and blink a lot."

Lindsay stayed behind with Daniel. "I tried to explain it to them, I really did."

"This is a disaster."

Lindsay chuckled.

"Why is that funny?"

"Two hours ago," she told him, "you were pretty sure they were going to entirely forget that they had promised to come."

"How do you know what I was thinking two hours ago?"

"Am I wrong?"

"No. I'm asking. How do you know what I was thinking two hours ago? You should start doing a mentalist act."

Lindsay laughed. "You're funny."

"Every morning I wake up hoping that's true."

"You want me to stay out here with you?"

"No. I stare into coffee cups and jot notes. Sometimes I pace a little bit. Go enjoy as much of the show as you can."

"What does that mean?"

"There are going to be hard-to-watch parts."

"Oh."

"And parts that are sexist. And racist."

"Really? Racist?"

"Yeah. Toby Lancaster is on the lineup. He thinks Don Rickles is a trailblazer."

"Oy."

"And Charlie Rosten does a straight twenty minutes of, 'I can say it cuz I'm black. Y'all say it, an' you'll get your asses kicked in the parking lot.' It's not pretty."

Lindsay blew a long, slow breath out, realizing just how long an evening she was in for. "Okay. I'll be sitting with Mom and Dad."

"Well that should be fun."

"It's fine. It's a show. We won't have to talk."

Daniel laughed. Lindsay left. Daniel jotted some notes in his spiral-bound notebook and wrapped his hands around the coffee cup. He looked down into the coffee.

Internally, he tried to run the set he had put together for the evening, but he never got much further than the opening line or two. Sometimes he imagined himself improvising a new joke or a new tag for a joke and jotted the thought down in his notebook. Other comics came in and chatted in pairs or trios in the bar awaiting their stage time. It always amazed him. He could not make small talk or friendly conversation in the time before he went on. Maybe that came with time and practice. Or with maturity. He needed to run his opening moments over and over again and worry that he wasn't running the whole set from top to bottom.

Once he got on stage, he was always okay, now. At first, he had been a trembling, struggling mess, but he'd done tens of workout spots here and down at the IMPROV in Hell's Kitchen and dozens of open mic nights. The worst of the panic had passed. Now it was just the weird freezing cold sensation beforehand. That and the need to turn inward and run his opening joke incessantly.

He sipped the coffee, accidentally poking his face with the little plastic stir stick. He chuckled. He pulled it from the coffee cup, tapped the last drips from it into his cup and practiced lining it up on a cocktail napkin the way he'd seen his father do so many times.

An hour or so into the show, Lindsay came out of the showroom. She sat down next to Daniel. She signaled the bartender and asked for an orange juice, accepting the offer of ice. She sipped through the plastic straw. Neither she nor Daniel looked at one another for a long moment. Neither she nor Daniel spoke. Then, when about half of her orange juice was gone, just after the bartender poured more coffee into Daniel's cup, he said, "They're not gonna make it, are they?"

Lindsay shook her head, a gesture Daniel easily picked up in the mirror behind the bottles.

"I told them not to come—"

"I know."

"—Until late in the evening."

"I know."

"Are they having fun at least?"

Lindsay said nothing. She might have shrugged, but barely if she did at all.

Daniel said, "Yeah. That's why I sit out here. There's a lot of . . ."

He trailed off, so Lindsay said, "Crap?"

"Yeah."

For a long while they didn't speak and then Lindsay said, "They're three, three and a half drinks in already."

"Jesus."

"And Mom heckled a guy."

"She did not."

"He said 'between you and I,' and she shouted the grammatical correction."

"Hank Rollins. Jesus. Does she not understand that the joke doesn't work if he gets the grammar right?"

Lindsay thought for a moment. "Wow. That's right. It wouldn't make any sense at all."

"I guess it's hard to hear the jokes when you're busy diagramming the sentences."

"If it makes you feel any better, they're trying hard to be good sports about it all."

"Yeah. That's what everyone wants from their parents. An earnest and tolerant attempt."

Lindsay laughed. "I should go back in. Try to slow them down a little bit on the drinks."

"It doesn't matter. Not if they're already gonna be gone by the time I'm up."

"Okay."

She signaled the bartender to find out what she owed for the orange juice. He said, "The kid's got it," and flicked a gesture toward Daniel. Lindsay went back into the show room taking the glass with what was left of her drink with her.

"I've got it?"

"You're workin' tonight. Yeah?"

"Yeah."

"You get two free drinks and I do free refills on your coffee, so I figured I'd save her the four dollars."

"Orange juice is four dollars?"

"All soft drinks are."

"Jesus. What are my parents spending on scotch tonight?"

"The scotches are your folks? Shit! I'll send 'em a round on the house."

"Please don't."

The bartender shrugged. "Whatever you want, Danny."

Daniel suddenly felt terrible about not knowing the bartender's name. He wrapped his hands around his coffee cup for warmth.

"Of course, that doesn't mean that tipping is discouraged."

"Shit. I'm sorry. Shit." For the first time ever, he pulled a five-dollar bill from his wallet and put it on the bar.

The bartender smiled and took the five. "Well done. No need to apologize. These are things they don't teach kids these days."

Daniel made a note in his notebook.

Laughter and applause leaked out of the showroom.

The primetime acts were up now, the established comedians with a TV credit or three on their résumés. Paul and Ellen wouldn't know who any of them were. They wouldn't know how impressive it was that their son was on the same bill with them. They would analyze these heroes of the microphone with the same jaundiced eye that critiqued the cadence of the local news readers, the grammar of the writers for *New York Magazine*, and the pro-military message underlying *Star Wars*.

Daniel put his pen to the notebook, but he didn't write anything. He wasn't sure what, yet, but there was something there in that memory. Sitting in the backseat of the station wagon, still riding the adrenalin high of witnessing—no, of *experiencing* that run down the trench with Luke Skywalker to blow up the Death Star, Daniel had listened resentfully as his parents in the front of the car dissected the film. It had taken his brain by storm, that space opera spectacular. The special effects were so far beyond the view screens and superimposed phaser blasts of *Star Trek*. That holographic chess board—he couldn't remember. Had the camera moved to pick up the three-dimensionality? It didn't matter. He had believed it so thoroughly that he had half convinced himself that it existed somewhere, on display in George Lucas' house perhaps.

He couldn't block out the discussion, though. Mom had said, "Well, that was just silly fun."

Dad had responded, "Really? I thought it was awful."

In the back Daniel had winced, knowing in general what was coming if not the exact form it would take.

"It was innocuous. I don't know why your jaw is all tense."

"Because—I'll tell you why, Ellen. Because everyone is so excited about this film like it's the greatest thing ever made. Kids are talking about it like it's their new religion and all I see is a return to nineteen fifty-seven with all those go-get-'em, heroes-on-the-battlefield, John Wayne movies. Instead of shouting ratatatat when they pretend to shoot each other, now they're shouting pew-pew-pew but it's the same fucking message."

"I just thought it was a retelling of the Arthurian legend."

"Sure. Sure, there was a lot of that easy, comforting, Joseph Campbell, heroes' journey bullshit, but mostly it was just good, old fashioned jingoistic American propaganda. Plucky rebels who can kill as many people as they need to because they're on the side of individual freedom against the dangerous monolithic army of nameless, faceless enemies who want to dominate for no clearly defined reason other than that they are bad."

Daniel spoke up. "Wait. I don't remember the good guys killing a lot of people."

"Really? How many people were aboard that Death Star the dumb farmer kid blew up? How many janitors and—and—and—navigators and—whatever? You think they were all there because they were evil and intent on subjugating strangers? Those were just people doing their jobs. All those white helmets with the slightly distorted voices. That's how propaganda works. Dehumanize an enemy, establish their ruthlessness and then you can do anything you want to as many of them as you want and people will cheer—they fucking *cheered*, Daniel—when you blow up a few hundred thousand of them in a spectacular, climactic set piece."

Daniel had rested his forehead against the glass of the window, looking out, trying desperately to hold on to just a little bit of his own opinion, trying not to admit that everything his father had said made sense, that he had been ready to cheer and had never thought of the implied lives lost.

Paul continued, assuming an instructive voice that masked a sense of urgency and political outrage. "This is exactly why they literally teach racism in the military. They refer to whomever is the enemy at any given time by slur and slur alone. That way they never have to feel as though they're killing people. It's easier to kill a Jerry or a Nip, a Gook or a Slope than it is to kill boys from Germany or Japan or Korea or Vietnam. Jesus. If this is the kind of movie people are going to now, we're gonna wind up right back where we were with a Republican in the White House and another round of flag-waving love-it-or-leave-it patriotism."

At Catch A Rising Star, the bartender asked Daniel if he was okay.

Daniel blinked.

The bartender said, "Usually when you pull out the notebook and the pen you write something. You've been sitting there like that for about an hour."

"What? I have?"

"No. But a couple of minutes."

"I was remembering something." He jotted down only, 'Star Wars—Car ride' and put the notebook away.

Shortly after ten, Paul came out of the show room. He said to Daniel, "Can you do something?"

"Sure. What do you need?"

Paul seemed confused, believing that his request had

been clear. "I mean about—you know—the show."

"Oh."

"I don't think half of these people are funny at all."

"And you want me to do something about that?"

"What?"

"Like—you want me to tell them to be funnier?"

"No. No. That's absurd. I just mean—I don't know how much more of this we can take."

"Okay."

"So, can you ask them if you can go up earlier so that we can see you before we leave?"

"That's not how it works, Dad."

"Let me just –" He waved to the bartender. He said, "Excuse me. What's your name?"

"Frankie," the bartender said, and Daniel made a mental note, then jotted it down in his notebook for good measure.

"Frankie, I'm Daniel's father."

"How are you, Mr. Grunman? Black label on the rocks, yeah?"

"Yeah. Listen, do you think you could move the list around, so Daniel is up sooner? I'm not really going to be able to stay that much longer. His mother and me. We have to leave pretty soon."

Daniel stared into his coffee cup. He wanted to cry. He also wanted to laugh.

Frankie said, "Um. What?"

"Don't get me wrong. It's a terrific show. Just terrific. I've been going to comedy clubs now and then since— jeeze. I saw Bob Newhart at the Purple Onion in San Francisco in '58."

"Wow."

"It's just that—we've really outgrown our night-owl days and we've had a few drinks. We're going to need to get back down to the apartment pretty soon, so I'd really appreciate it."

"You get that I'm the bartender, right?"

"Okay."

"I make the drinks. The booker makes the list and she leaves at six or six-thirty usually."

"So, who should I talk to?"

"Whom."

Paul blinked. He narrowed his eyes as though he'd been threatened and slowly went back into the show room.

Daniel said, "Frankie, I have never loved you as much as I do at this moment."

"I've seen your act. I knew how to shut him down."

"I feel like I didn't tip you enough."

"You tipped me fine, kid."

Daniel nodded. "Thanks." He focused on his coffee.

Frankie said, "Plus you finally learned my name. So that's two points for tonight."

Daniel blinked as Frankie refilled his coffee cup.

At eleven forty-two, Paul and Ellen came out together. Daniel had been aware of at least another two rounds of scotch going to them, so he was unsurprised that they seemed to be a little bleary, their balance a bit slurred. Ellen came to him and said, "I'm sorry, Honey. We just can't take any more. We're going to head home."

"Okay."

"We didn't realize it was going to be such a long night."

"All right."

"You want to come with us? You can share a cab."

"No. No, I have to stay. I'm performing."

"You're actually going to stick around forever, just for this?"

Paul said, "Ellen."

Daniel said, "Yeah. It's easier for me. You know. I haven't been drinking. Also, I get paid."

Ellen said, "Well it can't be much."

"No. It isn't much." He would be getting fifteen dollars for the late-night spot. He knew that his mother imagined something closer to a hundred. He did not disillusion her.

His father said, "Okay, Buddy. I'm sorry I couldn't get that taken care of for you." It took Daniel a moment to realize that his father was talking about his conversation with Frankie. Then Paul wrapped him in a hug and whispered scotchily into his ear, "You really don't have to do this if you don't want to." As he ended the embrace, he looked Daniel in the eye, trying to convey something that to Daniel only seemed to be, "I am considering napping in a cab."

"Why would I not want to do it?"

"I mean, you're so talented. This can't be the only way to get work as a comic. Maybe you should start with television or something."

"No. I think this is how it works." Then he said, "Is Lindsay going with you?"

Ellen said, "She said she wants to stick around, although I can't imagine why. A lot of these so-called comics are just awful."

"Could you not yell that in the bar at the club?"

Ellen slapped at his arm playfully. "I wasn't yelling, silly."

Paul said, "A little bit, you were."

"Sorry." Then in an exaggerated whisper she said, "So much vulgarity, they were using."

Daniel said, "Okay. Goodnight."

His father hugged him again, and again tried to convey something through psychic eye contact and then they left.

Daniel watched them go.

When he turned back to his coffee, Frankie was watching him closely. Daniel thought he might be considering offering him a drink. After a moment Frankie said, "You know you're funny, right?"

"What?"

"Just—when you talk about them in your act . . ."

Daniel didn't know where that thought was going, so he did not try to fill in the end of the sentence.

After a long moment of heavy silence, Frankie said, "I will bet you galoshes to gonads your sister is going to put a beverage through her nose if you do the bit about the scrabble game."

"I was a little bit nervous about them seeing that."

"Yeah. They left." Then, after a moment, he added, "And they're better when you do them than they are in person."

"Thanks?" He said it very much as a question.

"I don't know how you guys do it."

"Me and my sister?"

"No. You guys. All you comics. I don't know how you do it. All that . . . injury and you make it so funny."

Daniel's mind was back to his set now, focused on the opening moments, running the words in his head. He wasn't really following Frankie's meaning. He said, "I'm fine, Frankie."

Frankie put the bottle of Black Label back on the high

shelf where it belonged. He said, "You're really not, kid. But you will be. And that's what amazes me about you guys."

FUNERAL

"I don't understand," Lindsay said, but she lied when she said it. "Why would you want to ship her up there when all of her friends and her life are down here in New York?"

Michelle's mother, strained to irritability at the end of the phone, said, "Because we are her family and . . . this is how things are done. I don't need to explain myself to you, young woman."

"Okay. Okay, fine. Cape Cod, then. Will you let me know when the date is locked in for the service and the burial?"

Michelle's mother, Arlene, responded very quickly. "Oh, you don't have to come all this way."

"If you're not going to do it down here, I do."

Arlene sighed. "No. I mean. Your attendance is not required. It's very sweet of you to want to pay your respects, but the truth is, people don't travel to the funerals of their roommates."

"Roommates?"

"Yes. You two shared the place at—what was it?—that address that was just all numbers and letters."

"134 Avenue B, Apartment 12-c."

"That's the one. Yes."

"Yes. But we didn't think of ourselves as roommates. You know that. Right?"

"Oh, I'm aware that you were close. Yes. But that's not the point, really, dear."

"Isn't it?"

"This will really just be for family. You know."

"Yes."

"And maybe some close friends. You know, family friends and school friends from here on the Cape. That sort of thing."

"Yes. Could you let me know when that's going to –"

Arlene went on as though Lindsay had not spoken. "And I think a lot of these people, I mean, at least some of them might be uncomfortable having you there, knowing you were—well. You know."

"No. I'm not sure I do know. Say it aloud."

"That you were . . . close."

Lindsay said nothing. She let it hang on the line.

"That you . . . didn't . . . think of yourselves as roommates."

"So, you have friends and family who are uncomfortable with people who love one another showing up at each other's funerals."

"Let's not be unpleasant about this, shall we?"

"Mrs. Winter, I loved Michelle. We were together for two and a half years, lived together for almost two. I had planned to spend my life with her. She made me happy and much of the time I think I made her happy. I don't think I'm being unpleasant about this at all. Please. Would you—would you, please, let me know when you have the date set. I intend to be there for it."

"I don't want my daughter's funeral turning into some kind of political statement."

"Okay."

"This is not some fist-raising—I don't know—feminist solidarity event."

"Okay."

"People will be dressed well and respectful."

"I promise not to wear lumberjack plaid."

Arlene allowed that to hang heavy on the line for a moment.

"I promise to be as respectful as anyone. You know that I cleaned her up, right?"

"What?"

"Before the ambulance and the police got there, I cleaned her up. She shat herself when she went. Apparently, that happens a lot. I undressed her and cleaned her up and put her in clean clothes in the time between making the call and answering the door."

"Why are you telling me this?"

Lindsay was not certain of the answer to that. She had said it without thinking. She thought it had something to do with proving that she was respectful, but it was more than that. It spoke to the level of intimacy, to the level of commitment. That wasn't it either. She had wanted to curse, even if only in context. She had wanted to shock this clench-sphinctered wasp at the other end of the phone. She wanted to offend her without shouting "fuck." She said, "I want you to know that I did what I could to take good care of your daughter."

The woman made a grunting sound that Lindsay recognized as a sound Michelle had made from time to time, a sound that Michelle had made at moments that Lindsay's father or brother would have snorted. Arlene said, "Well, you certainly did a fine job of that, didn't you?"

The words stung, and Lindsay knew she had invited the attack with her gentle vulgarity. "Okay. Just . . . let me know so I can be there."

"You really just don't listen at all, do you? All you kids. Just do whatever you want with no regard for the people who might be affected."

"Is that what all us kids do?"

"I said as much to Michelle just last week. I said to her, 'I know you think you're romantic and rebellious but you're just making a fool of yourself, making the whole family look like a bunch of crazies with your shenanigans down there in New York.' I told her she was headed down a path that could only lead to heartbreak and then—she goes off and does this."

"You said that to her? A week ago?"

"Of course, I didn't know she was so unhappy at the time. Maybe I would have said something differently if I had known she was so fragile. But, of course, I'm not there, am I? I couldn't see her face or—I was just on the phone. It's so hard to pick up the signals when the only contact you have is long distance."

Lindsay felt her jaw tensing. She heard the accusation and could not quite tell whether it was intended. Her mind fumbled through the distinction between "implied," and "inferred," as a way to avoid the familiar rewind-and-replay of the last week's events. Her mind kept cycling through every recent interaction she'd had with Michelle, every conversation, every passing glance, every brittle-silence breakfast, passing one another in the small kitchen space, respecting the pre-coffee irritation of close quarters and half-shattered dreams. She had searched for the missed sign so many times she no longer knew what was memory and what was projection. She said, "Okay, Mrs. Winter. I'll see you in a couple of days or whenever."

Arlene said, "I'm serious. I would rather you not come."

Lindsay said, "Nonetheless."

She hung up.

The long drive from New York to Cape Cod gave Lindsay time to stew. By the time she made the transition from the I-95 to the 195 the rage had simmered to a nice thick seethe. A smooth reduction of resentment.

Michelle's younger sister Claudette had called to tell her of the service, and it had become clear in the course of the phone call that she had not done so out of respect for Lindsay's wishes, or even out of respect for Michelle's relationship. She had called because she knew it would piss off Arlene and Lawson, her parents. Like any good adolescent, Claudette had couched her action in self-righteous outrage, she had feigned a deep concern for the recognition of the relationship, but unconsciously she let slip the tell-tale turns of phrase that broadcast her disdain for the pairing. The expression, "life-style choice," came up, and "freedom to experiment," as the sorts of things she felt it was important to "tolerate."

The smell of the cardboard boxes in the back seat sometimes carried a slight scent of Nivea hand lotion, probably leaking a bit from the bottle in the gathering of Michelle's toiletries. Lindsay had collected almost all of her late lover's belongings and put them in boxes to return to the family, keeping only a few items that she just couldn't bear to let go. There was a necklace that Michelle had never actually given to her but that she had allowed her to wear frequently, often requesting that she wear it, saying that the sparkle of the stone set off her aura, an ironic jab at their friend Denise who read tarot cards and decorated her home in dream catchers of various sizes, wood and yarn constructs that, uncleanable, came to look over time like dust and hairball mobiles. Lindsay kept that necklace. She kept the hoodie that had once been her own but that she'd given to Michelle, who said she'd never owned a sweatshirt that didn't have a college or a club's name emblazoned on it. Michelle had made that her go-to running-to-the-store or answering-the-door-for-the-pizza-guy throw-on. She had worn it on Sunday mornings without a shower. It smelled of her in a way that made Lindsay feel like a safe and loving puppy when she put it on or just held it to her desperate nose. She kept that and intended never to wash it.

Everything else she had put into boxes to take back to Michelle's parents and, as she filled the boxes, she decided with a snide sort of smirk, that she would include the things they wouldn't expect. She included a half-empty box of tampons. She included a single sock with a hole in it that Michelle had used as a dust rag. *Fuck 'em,* she'd thought, throwing items into a box with aggression the recipients would never perceive, *let* them *throw out the personal trash.*

As the woods and the lobster roll shacks slipped by, Lindsay had conversations with an introjection of Michelle's mother, Arlene. She had conversations in which she railed at the woman for turning her grief into rage, for making it impossible to feel the loss and pain funerals are designed to serve because she was all caught up in the anger and defensiveness sparked by her prejudice. No. Bigotry. *Use the word,* she thought, indulging in the on-the-spot rewrites that only imagined conversations allow.

She thought wryly of the story she had heard about Walter Matthau who, after arguing with his wife through a tour of the famous death camp had snapped, "You ruined Auschwitz for me!"

The rural landscape gave way to cow pastures and then a small town's main street grew up around her with its store fronts and post office. People walked the sidewalk, parked their cars, seeming to have no idea at all that a beautiful young woman had taken her own life, leaving the world lost in its own hallways, barefoot and chilly and too big to hold hands but too small to cross the street alone.

Then a left turn took Lindsay's car into the stone walls and evenly mowed lawns of residential wealth. Where trees grew, they were carefully spaced in deliberately random-seeming arrangements so that wide slants of sunlight could bathe the lush grass where underbrush should have grown. Everything took on the hyper saturated look of an Ang Lee forest scene.

Her mind skittered back through conversational glimpses of Michelle's childhood. She began to understand the eyes through which her world had been perceived, the risk Michelle had taken and the courage she had shown. Lindsay felt wholly out of place in these surroundings. A small knot in her solar plexus wondered for the first time ever how much of Michelle's affection for her had been nothing more than rebellion against an oppressive upbringing of expansive privilege.

She immediately gave that small knot the voice of

Arlene and told it to shut up.

Wrought iron gates stood open and she drove through on the road that wound past headstones and soft landscaping toward the chapel. Several cars, all bigger and much cleaner-looking than her own, filled some of the paint-marked slots, but the parking area was far from full. Lindsay pulled into a spot just a little bit apart from the cluster of cars already there. She unfolded herself from the long drive and took a moment to stretch, turning her upper body from side to side to release her back. She rolled tension from her neck. She put one foot on top of the car and straightened the leg, pressing her chest to her knee, then she repeated the stretch with the other foot up. She let out a long slow breath, let out a soft snort that she recognized as her father telling her she was being silly, stalling in the parking lot after driving all this way to be here.

She climbed the three small granite steps to the entryway and went in, the stillness of the air inside striking her as a tactile reflection of the silence. She passed through the foyer and wondered if that part of a chapel had a specific name. She knew the benches were called pews. She knew something was called a rectory, but she didn't know what that was other than that it always made her think of men having butt sex 'cause of a joke she had once heard someone do about Priests and Alter Boys, years earlier when she'd gone to see her brother perform at a night club.

A woman stood at the doorway into the churchy part of the building, her back to the great space with the huge statue of Jesus looking sad and scary, arms outstretched and nailed up at the wrists, hands hanging limp as though a struggle to survive, an effort to escape was beneath his dignity. He seemed to be wearing a diaper and Lindsay's seething, inner voice muttered, *I'll bet he shat himself when he went.*

The woman at the doorway took a single step toward her, extending a hand. "Thank you for coming. Please take a moment to sign the guest book before you come in," Lindsay recognized her voice.

She said nothing, simply nodded and followed the woman's gesture. She went to the book and put her name in it and then wrote in the space for notes, "Michelle was the love I needed when I needed it. I do not remember life before her. I cannot imagine life without her." She stood for a moment, turning the pen between her fingers, wondering if there was more she should write. She set down the pen and headed inside to find a seat. A pew.

After she had time to go look at the name in the book, Arlene chased after her, brisk-walking down the aisle to where Lindsay was about to sit alone.

Arlene spoke in a very soft voice; her carefully maintained expression of polite grief made her lips move very little. "I thought I made myself clear when we spoke."

"Yes. You did." She spoke quietly, but not nearly as quietly as Arlene. She heard a slight echo, like the reverb effect on a cheap guitar amp. Some people toward the front of the . . . room turned to look.

Arlene hissed. "I am very uncomfortable having you here."

"I'm sorry I make you uncomfortable." She sat down.

Arlene crouched so she might continue to speak in that tiny whisper that remained impossibly audible. Clearly, she had a good deal of practice having private conversations in cavernous spaces. "This is a sacred space."

"I promise not to burst into flames."

Arlene gripped Lindsay's arm hard with a single hand and pulled her upright with a violent tug. She walked the younger woman back up the aisle. Lindsay had taken a few steps before she thought to pull away, but Arlene's hand had strength developed over years of tennis and golf. Her hold held.

She walked fast, and Lindsay stumbled once before she realized her options were to keep up or be dragged. She did not walk comfortably in heels to begin with, so the shoes chosen for their respectful femininity made the swift gait particularly difficult. She slowed for a quarter beat when they got to the . . . lobby? . . . but Arlene kept going and took her all the way out through the front door into the living air of the outside world.

Only when the doors had shut behind them did Arlene speak. "I don't know how else to say this, young lady. I do not want you here. My family does not need to have it rubbed in their faces at the funeral that my daughter ran off to do—whatever it is that you two were doing down there in New York City."

"Jesus Christ, you can't even say it, can you?"

"Watch your mouth!"

It took Lindsay a moment to figure out what she had said that could be considered inappropriate and when she did, she found she had no desire to apologize for it.

"You want me to say it? I'll say it. You should not be in this chapel because you're a pervert and a Jew, okay? Does it feel good to hear me say that? Does it make you feel superior to know that I'm one of *those* people with

47

traditional values and a family I want to protect from all the crazies and the criminals? I knew. I knew when she said she wanted to go to Sarah Lawrence College what she was thinking. I knew, and I just let it happen."

"Wait. You let what happen? Your daughter was wonderful. You know that. Right? She was . . . she was by far the best person I ever knew." Lindsay wiped tears from her cheeks but she wasn't certain what had drawn them out of her this time.

"She was such a bright and funny girl. And then . . . Just . . . look. You can watch the burial if you want but I really don't think you should be in the chapel. Okay? The service is about to start and I just want to grieve for my daughter. Is that okay with you? Is that all right? Do you *mind* if I just sit inside there and feel the . . . loss and the . . . the . . . I don't want to be angry. Not today. I don't want today to be about you and her and all the . . . lesbying."

Lindsay fought the urge to laugh, though she allowed herself a tight smile. It wasn't the confused verbing of the noun that got her. It was the sentiment, so close to the one she had imagined hurling at Arlene. She wanted to grieve without anger. She squeezed her nose and she snorted.

Arlene said, "What—was that?"

"Sorry. It's just—"

"Michelle did that. She did that when she visited last Christmas. Did she get that from you?" She mirrored the gesture.

Lindsay recognized it. She blinked. "I—she might have. I got it from my Dad, I think. I didn't even realize I'd picked it up."

Arlene grunted that odd little grunt.

"She used to do that, too."

"She used to do what?" and Lindsay noticed that, like Michelle, Arlene pronounced the airiness of the "wh" at the start of the word.

"That little grunty thing." She duplicated the sound.

"Did I do that? That's funny. It's something my husband does. I don't even really know what it means."

"It means you found something interesting or funny but don't want to admit it because it would feel like a concession of some kind."

Arlene grunted, then she chuckled. "There it is again!"

Lindsay nodded.

"Okay. So. You just—is this okay? You just wait out here and in about—I don't know—thirty, forty minutes we'll do the procession and you can be there for the burial?"

Her tone was so hopeful and so kind that Lindsay could see no way around it. Also, she had begun to feel as though her only purpose in going inside had been to put a thumb in Arlene's eye. She nodded. "Yeah. Okay."

"Thank you." Arlene took Lindsay's hand in both of her own and made eye contact as she said, "Truly. Thank you."

Lindsay nodded, and Arlene stood there a long additional moment not saying anything but, in her silence, a half-dozen other thank yous broadcast through her touch. *Thank you for understanding. Thank you for not hating me for my inability not to hate you. Thank you for not describing the way you had sex with my daughter. Thank you for giving my daughter joy in a way I couldn't approve of. Thank you for driving all this way even though I told you not to. Thank you for giving me this small win.* Then she walked inside, and Lindsay sat down on the cold, hard step to wait.

Distant echoing music came from inside.

Lindsay's ass went to sleep. She stood up, turned in small circles, waiting. She realized she could use the time productively, so she walked over to her car, opened the back and began carrying the boxes one at a time from her car and setting them down in a neat stack near the cluster of cars she correctly assumed belonged to Michelle's family.

Nobody in the chapel had looked like people who would have been her friends from school. They were all the age of Arlene and Lawson except for two girls Lindsay knew to be Michelle's sisters and one gangly young man that had to be the older brother, Kyle, who sat together in the front row.

As she carried boxes, she thought that perhaps she should have invited at least one or two of their friends to make the drive with her. It would have filled the space more and it would have blunted Arlene's sense that she was under attack. She felt guilty. She knew, though she hadn't known until now, that she had invited nobody to come with her because she did not want to blunt anything. She had come to her beloved Michelle's funeral intending her attendance as an attack.

Claudette emerged from the chapel and Lindsay recognized her as much by the adolescent affect as by the face she had seen in the rotating photographs on Michelle's screen saver. Michelle had come back from Christmas talking about how delightful Claudette and Delia were. She had described Claudette, saying that she had always been a serious and introspective kid but now she was so deep into her teens that she slouched around like a behemoth with an appointment in Bethlehem.

Claudette pulled a cigarette pack from her purse and lit it with an old-fashioned looking brass lighter. She walked toward Lindsay with a slight limp that she had clearly learned from wealthy young black men in Hip Hop videos. Lindsay snorted and set down a box.

Claudette watched her get another box and add it to the pile. She moved to Lindsay's car and looked inside. She saw that one box remained. She leaned against the car watching as Lindsay came back for the last box, and pushed the door closed with her butt. Then she walked with Lindsay as the woman carried the box across the parking lot and put it with the others. Only when Lindsay had set the box with the others did she say, "You need a hand?"

Lindsay snorted. "Funny."

"But you'll refrain from laughing in the interest of time."

"I'm trying to be respectful. It's a funeral."

"My mom was pissed."

"Yeah. Well. That's what you were going for, isn't it?"

Claudette raised her eyebrows as she dragged smoke into her lungs and blew it out through her young, perky nose. "Then she came back in from talking to you and she was . . . different."

"Yeah. I have that effect on people."

"Seriously?"

"No. I agreed to wait out here 'til the burial. Give her some space. She's grieving."

"So are you."

"Yeah. But I don't need to grieve with an invisible friend."

"I don't know what that means."

"I'm an atheist."

"Like Michelle."

"Yeah."

Claudette smoked. Lindsay smelled the smoke. It made her think of her parents. It reminded her of childhood and scrabble games and long rides in the back seat.

"Where do atheists go when they die?"

Lindsay thought about it for a moment. "I don't know. Where do atheists go when they die?"

"It's not a riddle. I'm asking."

"Oh! I don't—I don't think anyone goes anywhere when they die. We just go."

"So, you don't believe in life after death?"

"My grandfather said he believed in life after death, but that it's the life of other people who haven't died yet."

"Is that supposed to be funny?"

Lindsay shrugged. "Not today."

Claudette crushed her cigarette on the asphalt. Lindsay walked back to the steps and sat back down on the cold stone. Claudette sat down next to her. They sat in silence for a long time. "She wrote me a long letter about you once."

Lindsay wanted to see it. She wanted to read it. She stayed silent. She feared scaring the girl away if she showed any eagerness, as though she was waiting for a timid dog to come close. She looked out at the headstones beyond the parking lot. She kept her breath steady as if she had just bet big on a busted flush and hoped the guy in the cowboy hat would fold.

The guy in the cowboy hat folded. "It was a couple of weeks after she met you. She said she thought she had found the one. She said that she was more in love than she'd ever been. She said she was starting to believe in the possibility of joy and romance. It took her two pages to get around to the fact that you were a girl."

Lindsay nodded.

"She really loved you, I think."

"I really loved her."

"I like boys."

Lindsay nodded. "Okay."

"The boys I like piss my parents off as much as if I liked girls."

"Yeah, well. It's never easy."

"You know they threatened to cut her off, right?"

"What?"

"When she told my parents about you. They said they didn't want everything they'd worked for falling into the hands of the wicked."

Lindsay snorted. "Yeah. Wicked. That's me."

Claudette shrugged.

Lindsay said, "The wicked witch of the lower east."

"I don't know what that means."

"Don't worry about it."

"They didn't do it."

"Who didn't do what?"

"My parents. They didn't cut her off. Kept sending her money. Left her trust intact."

Lindsay nodded. She had known that Michelle got money from home, that she had come from money, but they'd never discussed the details.

"Even when she made you her inheritor and everything. They were furious. But they didn't cut her off."

Lindsay blinked slowly. She suddenly had a great many questions. She had a great many questions that she didn't want to ask. Her world tilted abruptly. She focused on the sensation of cold, smooth stone under her fingertips.

Two hours earlier she had filled her tank on a credit card, worried about how this trip on a weekday would affect her groceries budget. She had been forcing down thoughts of coming up short for rent and having to ask Mr. Norwalt for extra time to pay. She had wondered if she could go back to cleaning the studio in exchange for dance class instead of paying for it like a normal person.

She felt self-loathing rise like nausea and she fought the fantastic drift of imagined figures on a bank receipt.

She realized the pause had been too long, but she couldn't speak. The sudden shifts in circumstance had devastated her ability to compartmentalize. She'd been so angry that she didn't feel she could grieve properly. Then she'd let go of the anger when she realized that she was doing to Arlene exactly what she felt had been done to her and had found herself sitting alone. She had become calm and distant and practical. She had stacked the boxes neatly and had begun to think she had found closure in that act.

Now there was money. She didn't know how much, but it was more than she had. She felt rage growing again, a fury born of the idea that now she had to deal with what that gift might mean, the idea that now she had to feel hope and greed when she should feel only sorrow and loss.

Her hand had begun to tremble, fingertips barely touching the granite.

Claudette said, "So, it'll probably be fine. Right?"

"What?" She wondered if Claudette had been talking the whole time and she had been too involved in her own thoughts to listen, but she couldn't find a memory of words drifting by.

"They probably won't cut me off even if they don't like Keith."

Lindsay remembered abruptly that the girl was a teenager. "No. No. They probably won't. I don't know. I don't know anything."

"I should probably go back in before Mom notices I left."

Lindsay nodded. "Okay."

Claudette stood up. She shook each of her arms in turn to get her sleeves to fall right. "You gonna be okay out here?"

"I'm going to be okay."

"What are you going to do?"

"You know. Grieve."

"Do you need me to bring you some Kleenex or something?"

"No. No thanks. I have some in the car."

Later, when the family filed out, coffin carried by six men, two of them Kyle and a man she knew to be Lawson, Lindsay followed the group at a distance. She felt like an intruder at a garden party. A somber, boring garden party.

She noticed that Kyle's suit fit him perfectly, that in his late twenties he owned a tailored, bespoke black suit so spotless that he clearly only wore it on rare, solemn occasions. She wondered again how much money Michelle had left to her. She did not know how such details got handled.

Arlene dropped back from the group and walked with Lindsay in silence for a few steps. "If you'd like to join the family now, I think that would be appropriate."

"I'm okay. But thank you."

The men lowered the polished box into the ground a few yards away and then Lawson glanced toward his wife and she waved him off with a small gesture that said, 'It's okay. I've got this,' but looked to Lindsay as though it might mean, I am petting the head of an imaginary standard poodle but hope nobody notices.

Arlene said, "Do you mind if I stand back here with you for a bit?"

"No. That's okay."

They stood in silence.

"You know she had a will?"

"Claudette told me. I don't really know how any of that works."

"Our lawyer will take care of it. He'll get in touch."

"Can you—Can you just contribute whatever she left me to . . . something good? Suicide prevention or . . . you know . . . LGBT rights or something?"

"I'm afraid not. It has to go to you. What you do with it is . . ."

Lindsay nodded. Eventually she would learn the number. She would have to find out what Michelle had risked for love. She would have to make decisions when the money was real, when the money was in her hands, when nobody was watching.

She realized she was hungry and tried to remember when she had eaten last.

Arlene said, "Will you do one thing for me?"

"I thought I already did."

Arlene looked at the ground then, self-conscious. Maybe ashamed. "Right. Right." She blew a long breath out through pursed lips and Lindsay could see the wrinkles around the woman's lips formed over years of long breaths blown through those pursed lips, deep grooves she tried to disguise with makeup.

"What do you want me to do?"

"Just—whatever you do with the funds, hold out enough to live on for a year or two." Her eyes twitched as though a bright light had startled her. "Michelle told me you had important auditions coming up, that things are . . . changing for you right now. Don't let anything distract you from that."

Lindsay wondered how much Michelle had talked about her with Arlene. She wondered what Arlene had thought of in that moment that she squinted and then recovered her composure. She wondered how much money it has to be before it's called 'funds'.

She said, "That's something you want me to do for you?"

"Yes. For me. For Michelle. For me."

They stood silent for a long moment.

Arlene said, "I'm sorry I . . . grieved at you."

Lindsay chuckled. "Yeah. Me too."

"I wanted to be a dancer," but the tiniest imaginable pause before the word 'dancer' made Lindsay think it was something else that Arlene had wanted to be. She said, "I should go do the . . ."

People were taking turns grasping a shovel and tossing dirt into the hole.

"Okay. Yeah."

"The older I get, the more time I spend throwing dirt."

"It's okay. I get it."

"I'm burying my daughter and doing word games. I don't know what's wrong with me."

"Do you want to know one of the first things Michelle

told me about you?"

"That I didn't love her? I think she always thought I didn't love her."

"She never said that. I don't think she thought that."

"I was so afraid that's what you wanted to drive up here to tell me."

"No."

"What did she say?"

"She told me you were always ready to be taken aback by some effrontery."

Arlene chuckled. "Word games."

Lindsay nodded.

Suddenly Arlene was hugging her and she was wrapped in someone else's mother's arms, drowning in unfamiliar perfume and soft, soft fabric. Arlene said, "I loved her in spite of it all. You know that, don't you?"

"I do, Mrs. Winter. I do know that."

She knew what 'in spite of it all' meant, but she could not find anger at the words. She did not hear an attack. She heard an apology. She heard a confession. She heard anguish that hoped it could echo through the corridors of her love to be perceived by a kind, beautiful dead woman in an imagined afterlife.

NOSTALGIA

Daniel stopped for the light at the corner of Hollywood and Highland where actors dressed up damply as superheroes to pose for tips with disappointed tourists. Waiting to cross the street with a cluster of mere mortals, Superman stood on the curb. He was a particularly convincing Superman, well enough built to wear the jersey knit costume without fake padded cartoon muscles built into it. His bootblack hair reflected the streetlights like ink on a high-gloss page and the one comma of curl dipped down over his brow just as it should.

Standing nearby, a young boy held his mother's hand and saw Superman standing, waiting with them. He might have drawn his mother's attention to the Man of Steel, but he did not.

Daniel imagined that the boy did not want to hear what she thought of the spectacle in red and blue. He wanted to have this moment of overlap between fantasy and reality to himself, unbroken. An unknown observer, seeing the scene like a moviegoer, Daniel watched the beats play out like the frames of a silent movie.

The iconic hero looked down at the boy and the boy

looked up at him. Superman smiled, half winked and then the light changed. For a breathless moment, it almost seemed that as the crowd moved across the street, Superman might raise a guiding fist to the sky and lift into the evening air to vanish into a primary-colored point in the distance, but he did not. He walked across the street, as did those around him. As the group thinned, stretching across the roadway, the boots of his costume came into view, scuffed and blackened by the Hollywood boulevard filth.

As Daniel passed the man in the costume, driving on down toward the small theater in which he would tell jokes about President Reagan, about the importance of truth, the nature of memory and the magic of language, he experienced an odd sensation, a nagging sense of loss to which he could not quite put a name but which he knew to be familiar and worthy of further exploration. It seemed that something important had happened.

He needed to figure out just what it was. He needed to remember when he had felt it before, it seemed, and everything would come into focus.

He opened his window just a crack and pulled the small carved-wood pipe from his ashtray. He felt with his thumb to ascertain that there was still some pot mixed with the ash in the bowl. He licked carbon off his thumb, put the pipe between his teeth and put the flame of a butane lighter to the bowl. He drew the sharp smoke into his lungs as he drove on past Fountain Avenue, hoping to reach that rare and wonderful state of lucidity in which dream and imagining and memory all melt together. As he turned onto Melrose, he remembered a childhood joy.

He remembered coming home late at night with his

father from a movie or one of the student plays at the college. He remembered dozing in the front seat of the car, warm from the heater's blow, face cool against the glass of the window. He remembered being awake enough to know that he was dreaming, that he was on his way home, but asleep enough to be completely relaxed, heavy in the swaying, vibrating momentum of the journey. He would feel the slowing shift from highway to road, the last, familiar turns and then the rocking stop of arrival.

Knowing the travel was at its end, he would pretend still to be soundly asleep. His father would lift him from the back seat in his arms to let him remain in slumber, though Daniel knew he was faking and perhaps Paul did, too. He was too big to be regularly carried by then, though, too heavy, too capable. So, he would pretend to sleep, and he would smell the nicotine and the antiperspirant, and he would feel the rough beard growth of his father's cheek against his own. He would allow his father to carry him and he would allow himself to feel safe and protected in a way that had been lost to him years or maybe only months earlier.

When they reached the stairs, though, his father had set him down. He had put Daniel on his feet, and he had said, "Sorry, kiddo. You've gotten too big. You're on your own from here."

Just that fast the comfortable ride was over. Worse still, he had been swept up in shame realizing that his father had known the deception the whole time, that they had been complicit in a lie. Had his father been enjoying the pretense too, or had he just been indulging Daniel's desire? And if Daniel had been awake, he wondered as a child, why had he wanted so badly to be carried? Why did it make him want to weep that he had to walk up the stairs himself as he did every night?

He pulled the car into the Fred Segal parking lot and waved to the valet kid, letting him know that he was a performer and would not have to pay to park. He took the last hit from the pipe and turned the image over in his mind, revisiting the time in his father's arms and enduring that moment of disappointment at the foot of the staircase anew with each review of the experience.

He did not know as a child that what he was experiencing was his first taste of nostalgia and then nostalgia denied. He did not have that vocabulary, yet. He did not have that much self- awareness, reveling in the pretense that he could reclaim a simpler time when he was less self-reliant, when he felt better protected, safer. As a child he had not known that even that simpler time was a distortion of memory, that when he had been smaller and more often carried, he had yearned to walk on his own, to learn self-reliance, to escape the coddling of toddlerhood. He only knew that he felt warm and comfortable in the arms of his father, hearing him groan as he lifted the growing weight and that he must pretend to sleep to enjoy it.

He sat in the car, luxuriating in memories of flopping in his father's arms. He longed to hold on for just a moment more to that beautiful fantasy.

It melted though, first from memory to fantasy and then sublimating in a vapor of melancholy. He knew against all his powers of desire that he was not a child in his father's arms but an adult alone in a car, dead broke and almost out of grass. To pretend to be anything else was a lie and the truth held him fast, insistent, holding a power of its own more important than any comfort provided by a soothing lie. All nostalgia, he realized, depended upon a lie, a willful ignorance of the fact that life was always as complex as it is now, even if we were not yet equipped to perceive it.

There it was again. That feeling. That sense of unnamable, barely bearable loss.

Using both of those moments, the heartbreaking desire to remain in a moment of double-ply memory and the sad-startled flash of filthy red boots on the mortal in the superhero costume, he was able to bring vocabulary to bear. Those moments served as the spaced lenses of a telescope, allowing him to see clearly through the distortions of time, across the deceptive vastness of the mind, to the shameful, human heart of the matter.

The simplicity of it, once he had seen it, seemed as obvious, as clumsy, as utterly without subtlety as the six-panel, four-color tales of the comic books he had once loved so much. It was the sadness of a grown man who, just for a moment, lowered his guard and allowed himself to believe.

HAIR

Ellen leafed through the magazines on the little coffee table in the waiting area. She imagined herself wearing the clothes of the celebrities on the pages. She imagined herself turning, cameras flashing, smiling with effortless grace. She shook her head dismissively.

She stood up. "Tammy?"

Tammy put a finger up to the woman whose hair she was cutting, signaling her to stop speaking for a moment. "What's up?"

"Do I have time to step outside for a cigarette while I wait?"

"Absolutely. You know you're early, right?"

"Am I?"

"I have you down for twelve thirty."

"Yes. What time is it now?"

"Twelve twenty, now."

"I like to be punctual."

"I'll be ready for you at twelve thirty."

"I'm going out for a cigarette then."

"Okay."

"You're not allowed to smoke inside anywhere

anymore."

"I'll be ready in about ten minutes."

"We used to just smoke anywhere. Movie theaters. Airplanes. Offices."

"Yeah. Plenty of time."

"Can you believe it's been forty-five years?"

"What has?"

"That I've been smoking."

Tammy allowed her focus to shift back to the work at hand, pulling the comb through her client's hair, trimming the extended ends.

"I don't feel old enough to have been smoking for that long."

Tammy surreptitiously rolled her eyes in the mirror at the woman in her chair. The woman suppressed a smirk.

"You'd think I started smoking when I was eleven, right? I mean, that's because of you, of course. It's the hair that gives me that youthful sparkle!" She laughed.

"If you want to get that cigarette in before I'm ready for you . . ."

Ellen said, "Right. Right. Right you are."

The door made its little jangly sound as she stepped outside. She wrapped her long coat tighter around herself irritably as the wind slipped through the loose weave of Boston's streets. She cupped a hand around her plastic lighter as she put flame to tobacco. The flame blew out twice before she realized she could turn her back to the wind for better cover. She drew the first pull of smoke into her lungs.

She studied the parked cars, the absurdly expensive ones that seemed, as always, to be recently washed, the filthy old junkers that some people drove around in with no seeming self-consciousness at all, covered in years of city grime, back seats littered with old fast food bags.

She wondered if she looked elegant, standing on the sidewalk, cigarette in one hand, the other tucked into a pocket. She chuckled at the thought. *Imagine me,* she thought, *looking elegant when I'm really just out here to smoke before a haircut.* She turned into the chill wind so that it would properly blow her overgrown hair back instead of just messing it up and driving it across her face.

A delivery truck pulled up at the building next door and a young man got out and carried a package inside. He glanced at her and gave a friendly nod. She waved with her left hand so that he could see her wedding ring.

When he came back out, he didn't seem to notice her, so she said, "You must be freezing."

Startled, he turned. "What's that?"

"I can't believe you're out in shorts in this weather."

"Oh! I'm fine. I'm used to it."

"Ah, youth!" Ellen said with the inflection that made it witty.

The man waved and nodded again as he got back into his truck and drove away.

It was nice, the interaction. Small, but nice. No matter how old she got, Ellen enjoyed feeling attractive, having young men flirt with her like that.

She crushed out her cigarette on the sidewalk and pushed back inside.

Tammy swept the floor around her chair as the previous client settled up with the woman at the reception desk. "Slide on in. I'm all ready for you."

Ellen slipped out of her coat, hung it from a coat tree that served to display handmade scarves the salon sold. As

Ellen took the big chair that faced Tammy's mirror, Tammy signaled the receptionist with a subtle tilt of the head so that she would move the coat to one of the hooks near the door that were there for that purpose.

Tammy stood behind Ellen and talked to her via the reflection as she ran her fingers through the woman's hair, exploring its length and texture. "What are we doing today?"

"Oh, the same as always. Go fairly short. You know. Not like a nineteen twenties flapper, you know but . . . what's it called?"

"Short?"

"Yes! I think Paul likes it more when it's short. Can you do—You know. What do you call that haircut that looks like-" She gestured in a way that was intended to define a desired shape but seemed to indicate that she was trying to put on an imaginary motorcycle helmet. "You know what I mean?"

"Um."

"That thing that makes you look like an adorable elf."

Tammy laughed. "A pixie cut?" She snapped a nylon poncho around Ellen's neck.

"Yes! Is that what that's called? I like that. A pixie cut."

"We can do that."

"Of course we can! I have faith in you."

"Good to know. Okay. Wash first?"

"Oh, that's not necessary. I took a shower before I left the house this morning."

"All right." She shpritzed water onto Ellen's hair from a plastic squirt bottle.

"We just got a new shower head. It's incredible. It has all these different settings. It can be a gentle rain or a pounding massage or—oh—just whatever you like. It's really extraordinary."

"Is it on a hose?"

"What?"

"Is it the kind you can use hand-held? On a hose?"

"Oh, no. Nothing like that." She paused for a moment thinking about it. She said, "That would be lovely, though."

Tammy began combing out Ellen's hair. She pulled it back. She pushed it forward. She examined it in the mirror.

"I might never get out of the shower."

Tammy laughed.

"Just think of the things you could do with that."

"Yeah. Got it."

"Right?"

Tammy nodded. She began cutting Ellen's hair.

Ellen said, "I didn't write that."

"What?"

"That joke. I can't take credit for it."

"What joke?"

"I might never get out of the shower."

"Okay."

"I went to see my son at a nightclub once doing one of his stand-up comedy skits and one of the comics saw a woman laughing in the front row and he said, 'When you laugh you put your head right in your lap,' then he said, 'If I could do that, I would never leave my house.' It's really the same joke."

"Yeah. I don't think he wrote that joke, either."

"Don't they have to?"

"What?"

"I don't think they're allowed to just go up and do jokes

other people have written. You know. Unless they paid for them."

Tammy shrugged. "How was your son?"

"What?"

"Your son. You said you were there to see him perform . . .?"

"Oh. We didn't stay. It was a long night. This was back in New York. It wasn't a big deal show. It was just a showcase club, you know? One comic after another, all night long."

"Okay."

"Some of them had a funny joke or two but most of them . . . just . . . yech."

"You know who I enjoy? I like Eddie Izzard. I think he's very funny."

"Is he the weird guy who always looks constipated?"

"I don't know who that is?"

"Oh, yes you do. He's very funny."

Tammy shrugged apologetically. "No. He's British and he's a transvestite and he's really smart. I think he's a certifiable genius."

"Oh! I'll have to look into him. Is he on the internet?"

Tammy nodded.

"Lizard?"

"No thank you. I've eaten."

"What?"

"Izzard. Eddie Izzard."

Ellen nodded. "I'll remember that." Then, after a moment, "'No, thank you. I've eaten.' That's funny."

"Thank you. I'm pretty sure I didn't write it."

Ellen watched in the mirror as the scissors darted, a hummingbird snapping about her ears. "I've thought about it, though."

Tammy kept working. She did not bother to ask. She knew the thought would play out.

"Writing jokes. I think I'd be very good at it. I used to write poetry and I think it's a lot the same."

"Huh," trying to remain engaged in the conversation but uncertain as to what direction it was now taking.

"Economy of words is the key, I think. Not saying too much, giving just enough information and then letting it go. You know what I mean?"

"I never really thought about it."

"I was pretty good. Got three pieces into *The Pages* when I was at Barnard."

"What's that?"

"It's a college. I did undergrad there."

Tammy laughed. "No. *The Pages*. I don't know what that means."

"Oh! That was a magazine. Short fiction. Poetry. That sort of thing. It wasn't a big deal. But at the time . . . I was so excited. I still have a few copies somewhere."

"That's very cool. I didn't know you were published."

"Oh, I wouldn't say that I'm published."

"You just said . . ."

"It was a long time ago. And it was a small magazine. I don't think it's even still in print."

"Do you still write?"

"I haven't had time. It's fine though. I thought I'd be able to be a wife and a mother and still write but I'm happy with the choices we made. I made. I love my kids, and they both turned out terrific and they both picked up the writing gene, too. So that's kind of like I'm writing all the time. Right? Kind of?"

Tammy mussed up Ellen's hair and then combed it down again, examining her work.

"I think about it, though." She sighed. "I used to sit at that manual typewriter, roll in a sheet of paper and just . . . tell the truth. It wasn't really all that difficult for me. Just all the thoughts and ideas that ran around in my head, tickety-tackety out onto the page and then people really liked them. One professor said that I had a real knack for it. He said he had never seen anyone reveal so much of their inner life without lapsing into self-conscious irony."

"Wow."

"I never really knew what he meant, but I took it as a compliment."

Tammy nodded.

"I liked him a lot. He was one of my favorite teachers. I think he found me very attractive, but I really didn't think of him in that way. You know? He was in his thirties and he seemed so old to me. Can you imagine?"

"I used to think—"

Ellen went on. "I remember knowing that if I wore a skirt and sat in the front row, he would get flustered. But it didn't matter. By then I'd met Paul and we were pretty much going steady."

"'Pretty much going steady?'"

"Oh, I don't know what it's callcd now. Going out. You know. Dating."

"No. Got that. It was the 'pretty much,' I was asking about."

"He was . . . working some things out. He wasn't sure about me. Well. Not just me. All of it. You know." She made a gesture that was meant to make clear what 'all of it' was but just seemed to imply that she needed to get cobwebs unstuck from her fingers.

A brief sadness crossed her face and Tammy saw it in the mirror but decided not to ask what it meant, where it had come from.

Tammy brushed hair from Ellen's smock and then unsnapped it and folded it aside in a gesture so practiced it was automatic. She fluffed Ellen's hair with her fingers a last time and then used a blow dryer to clear away any remaining clippings from her shoulders and face.

Ellen said, "You're a wonder, kid!" She liked to be encouraging, to let people feel good about themselves when they were around her. It was nice to have good friends like Tammy that she could talk to.

Tammy held up a hand mirror behind Ellen's head. Ellen examined herself admiringly, but not particularly closely. She had no criticism.

LAYOVER (ONE)

Daniel thanked the waiter for the cup of coffee. He peeled back the foil from a tiny plastic container of half and half and poured it into the dark liquid. He watched it disappear into the warm depths before using the spoon to stir with gentle circles and distribute the cream until the coffee took on the overall tone of a rich Mediterranean suntan.

Distant P.A. systems echoed down the corridors announcing flight delays, gate changes, final boarding.

His father's plane had been scheduled to land just a few minutes earlier. Daniel had arrived early enough to find the Daily Grill, order coffee, get the coffee and stir in the cream before he saw Paul coming toward him, smiling.

Tom Bradley International Terminal at LAX provided stores and restaurants in the area outside the security-checked spaces accessible only to ticket holders. The undertone of disoriented tension carried by travelers, the hello- or goodbye-anxiety of those dropping people off or picking them up, the subtle hostility of airport police, and the fragile behavior of families with small underage kids always on the verge of meltdowns all combined to transform the generic store fronts and chain restaurants into an overpriced mall of the damned.

His father seemed, as always, to be limping a little bit. His carry-on bag hung from his shoulder like the oversized purse of a 1970s disco queen. His smile projected joy at seeing his son along with a sheepish apology for having to meet so briefly at the international terminal during a layover.

As he approached, Daniel stood up to welcome him with a hug. He spread his arms wide for Paul and announced, "Firm embrace!" The narrative mannerism was one he'd copied from a Mel Brooks appearance on a popular television sit com, but he was quite certain it was not something his father would recognize. His parents lived in a tightly controlled academic bubble. Looking out through the iridescent dish soap lens of intellect, they gazed at a world cleansed of frivolity, of hopelessness, of mindless entertainment. They prided themselves on an utter ignorance of popular culture.

Paul slipped into a chair at the table and asked, "Did you order for me?"

"Didn't know what you'd want."

"Same as always. Jameson on the rocks. Or scotch."

"That's kind of what I thought, but for a while there you were limiting yourself to red wine."

"Yeah. That didn't really last very long." Paul raised a hand to get the attention of a waiter.

After he had ordered they sat silent for few moments. Daniel turned his coffee cup slowly on the tabletop by pushing the little handle with a fingertip.

"You're not drinking at all?"

"I have to drive," then, after a short pause, "I don't

really drink much, ever."

"Some kind of a problem?"

"Nah. Just—I smoke a lot of pot and talk about marijuana legalization on stage."

"I don't understand." He half-nodded acknowledgement as the waiter put a drink down for him.

"If I smoke pot and talk about that, and I drink too, then I'm just a partier who likes to be wasted. I want it to be very clear that it's a preference, that I have a drug of choice."

"I don't always understand what you're doing."

"I know."

Paul used his fingertips to turn his drink on top of his cardboard coaster.

"You do that too. I never noticed I'd gotten that from you."

"What?"

Daniel said, "Turning the glass."

Paul snorted. "I tell people I had no mannerisms until you were born and then I started co-opting all of yours."

"I strongly suspect I did not emerge from the womb squeezing my nose."

"I only do that when I'm in public and I realize I was about to pick it."

"Yeah. I don't like to admit that. It's not my most appealing attribute."

"I'm your father. You're not required to be appealing."

Daniel shrugged.

"Do you have a show tonight?"

"No. Why?"

"You seem awfully dressed up for drinks at the airport."

"Coffee."

"Right."

"My manager said I should always be on brand when I'm out in public."

"On brand."

"Yes."

"I don't always understand what you're doing."

"I know."

Paul sipped. Daniel sipped. They both circled their memories trying to remember all the things they had wanted to talk about while they had this little bit of time together.

Paul said, "But you're okay, though. Yeah?"

"Yeah," Daniel lied.

"No?"

"I don't always understand what I'm doing."

"I can't tell you how much of a relief that is to me."

Daniel wanted to ask what that meant. He did not.

That did not stop Paul from answering. "You give the impression that you know exactly what you're doing, that everything is calculated, planned. It makes me very uncomfortable."

"You hate outlines."

"Exactly!" Paul enjoyed being thoroughly understood from time to time. "They're the death of spontaneity."

"I know. That's why I mentioned it."

"I find it comforting to know that you're as uncertain as the rest of us."

"Glad my terrifyingly tenuous existence can provide you some comfort."

Paul nodded. "Now we're getting to it."

Daniel squeezed his nose. Then he chuckled, realizing

the mannerism had reminded him of one of the things he'd wanted to discuss with his father. "I've stopped doing cocaine entirely."

"Were you snorting a lot?" Something about the way he emphasized the word 'snorting' suggested an utter lack of familiarity with the word.

Daniel knew that Paul had done cocaine from time to time over the years. The faculty cocktail parties had been awash in booze, hazy with smoke and sometimes ran late into the night with self-certain, overconfident, long-winded monologues delivered by various tense-jawed, fast-talking hyper-intellectuals. "Not a lot. I could never really afford it. But more than I should have. I realized I was spending time with people I didn't really like 'cause I thought they might be holding."

Paul nodded, but he said nothing.

"I think you know I used to hang out with Sam Kinnison."

"I don't know who that is."

"Was." And then, "I gave you one of his albums. Before everything went to CDs."

"Oh. Yeah. The fat one."

"Yeah. He was heavy."

"Screams a lot."

"Screamed."

"Right. I hate his stuff. It's very angry and—ultimately reactionary if I'm remembering it right."

"Yeah."

"He died?"

"Yeah."

"I'm . . . sorry?"

Daniel shrugged. "When you eat and snort as much as

Sam did, you have to measure your life in pig years."

Paul did not laugh. He waited.

"We weren't really close. I thought we were. But . . . we weren't really close. I was at the outermost edge of his entourage. It made me feel like I was really part of the comedy scene but . . . I was just partying with people who didn't want to hear what I had to say."

"I don't know what we're discussing right now."

"I keep trying to do all the stuff that made my heroes my heroes and it keeps not leading me to where I want to get. I go to the right parties. I sleep with the right women."

"Who are the right women?"

"Most of them."

"I don't think that's how you get there. I think where you want to get can only be a by-product of doing really good work."

"I think that's a myth. I think that's an East Coast fantasy that revolves around an obsolete belief in an artistic meritocracy."

"I hate to think that's true." He took a breath that indicated he was about to say more but then waved off the thought, inviting Daniel to ask what he had been about to say.

Daniel recognized the breath-and-wave mannerism as it was one of his own. He obliged. "What?"

"I just—I don't understand why you feel you should be rewarded for a life of hedonism."

"I like to think that a life of hedonism is its own reward."

Paul chuckled. "That's funny. You use that on stage?"

"No. I just said that in response to . . ." He thought about it for a moment and then said, "I'm not at all certain that'll work on stage."

"You probably have a better ear for that than I do."

Daniel nodded.

"But you're alright though, yeah?"

Daniel wanted to say that he was not okay. He wanted to tell his father that he was a month behind on rent and that he wanted to break up with his girlfriend, but she had supported him for six months and he felt indebted. He wanted to tell his father that he had so little in his bank account that he couldn't make a withdrawal from an ATM. He wanted to cry. He wanted to be held. He wanted to be invited to come back to the East Coast and live in his old room and be taken care of. "Yeah. Yeah, I'm all right," he lied.

Paul squinted for the amount of time it would have taken him to blink. It was a micro expression that meant he had spotted the lie and decided not to call it out. Daniel recognized it from his own face. He recognized it from the mirror, from the moments when he was shaving and caught himself pretending that he was a successful comic because he had a gig coming up in a month or pretending that he was a successful writer because he had pitched a script two weeks earlier. Paul said, "Good. Good. I worry." Then, after a brief pause, "I should probably get going pretty soon. The security line for international flights can get long."

Daniel nodded. "Yeah. Okay."

Paul sipped his drink. "You need a couple of dollars for parking?"

"Nah. I got it." He pulled out his wallet and slowly brought out his Visa card.

"I've got the drinks, kiddo."

"I can buy."

"Nah. I got it."

They made eye contact, Daniel making sure his father had intended to mimic his mannerism, Paul wanting to be certain that Daniel knew it had been deliberate.

Daniel allowed his father to buy him coffee. It was a relief. He had not been at all certain that card would have gone through.

PLAN

Lindsay pinched a bit of green, sticky bud from the plastic baggie and stuffed it into the bong's bowl. She took a moment to smell the tips of her fingers before reaching for the lighter. "I can't believe you can actually pay for this place just by doing your comedy shows."

"If I wanted someone to take pot shots, I'd go visit Mom and Dad."

Lindsay, pulling smoke through the gurgling water, put a finger up asking for a moment to finish the hit. She lifted her thumb off the carb and pulled in the chamber smoke with a hiss and then held her breath for a moment before squeaking out through a closed throat, "I meant it wholly as a compliment. I didn't mean, 'I can't believe you make money,' or 'I can't believe you support yourself,' I meant 'I can't believe how cool my little brother is.'"

"Oh. Well, in that case, I don't think I can argue with you."

"And why would you want to, really?" She let the smoke out slowly, refusing to cough.

"I want to ask a question."

"Okay."

"I don't want you to think I'm being a dick."

"Okay."

"Seriously. You know how . . . a minute ago I thought you were attacking me when you weren't?"

"Yeah. No. I totally get that. I'm really sorry. That's not what I meant."

"I know. But—I'm saying, I don't want you to hear this the way you would hear it coming from Dad. I want you to know that it's just a question."

"Two more days, I think."

"What?"

"You want to know how much longer I'm staying on your couch. I'm saying I think I'll be gone in two days."

"Seriously?"

Lindsay grinned and nodded, pulling another hit into her lungs.

"You're going back?"

Lindsay did cough now, but it was more of a pot smoker's spit take than a reaction to the dry heat. "Oh, fuck no. I'm staying. I should hear tomorrow that I got the apartment I want."

"Wait. Wait. You found an apartment? When did you find an apartment?"

Lindsay grinned at him.

"So . . . you're staying! Here. I mean. Not here, but here."

Lindsay nodded. "It's January and I wore a tee shirt and shorts to go out for coffee today. How could I *not* stay here?"

Daniel nodded, understanding. "The weather's good but . . . What are you going to do? I mean . . . do you have a plan? Or . . . do you . . . have a plan?"

Lindsay laughed. "Now you sound a lot like Dad."

"Sorry. Yeah. I get that. But . . . do you?"

"Have a plan?"

"Yeah."

"Sort of. No. But if I went back, I'd be not having a plan in the cold, far away from you and very close to Mom and Dad."

They sat for a moment, comfortable in one another's company. Daniel looked at his hands. He scratched at a cuticle with his thumb nail. He said, "It's not easy here, Linds."

"It's not easy anywhere."

He shook his head. He did not want to confess but he did not want to be part of the Los Angeles lie. "Nothing is what you think it is. Seriously. Everything they told us, everything we learned about a life in the arts. It's not what it's supposed to be out here."

"You're doing okay."

Daniel closed his eyes for a long moment. "I'm not. I'm really not, Lindsay."

"Look at this place! Are you kidding me?"

He stood up. He went to the window and looked out even though both he and Lindsay knew there was nothing to look at out there but the little parking lot, nearly empty in the middle of a weekday. "I'm broke all the time. Like . .. all the time."

Lindsay took off her glasses. She cleaned them with the sleeve of her tee shirt and tilted her head to the side watching Daniel's back. She knew there was something more in what he was saying, something secret. The sadness in his neck tension ran deeper than simple money woes. "You're a twenty-four-year-old comic. I think you're supposed to be broke."

Daniel shook his head, still looking out at the parking lot. "No. No, that's part of the lie they tell us. On the East Coast. In school. You dedicate yourself to the art. You work your craft. You pay your dues. You keep your head down. People notice. Nobody notices, Lindsay. Nobody cares. I'm doing twenty, twenty-five weeks on the road this year. That's what I've got booked. Weekends, one-nighters in between. I'm doing the work. I'm keeping my head down. I'm funny as hell and I'm writing. All the time. Spec scripts. Screenplays. You have no idea."

"You write beautiful stuff, kiddo."

"Yeah. Right? I write beautiful stuff! But you know who's not broke all the time? Comics who put together a tight six minutes that they can do on television about airline food and bad dates. Innocuous observations that don't threaten anyone—those'll get you a sit com deal. Writers who don't know how to put together a scene but have a knack for pitching their ideas. People with agents. People with agents who their parents introduced them to. You know what the last agent I met with said to me?"

"No."

"This was a literary agent. Which, in Hollywood by the way has nothing to do with literature. He looked at a couple of my scripts 'cause I was recommended by someone who works on *Dear John*."

"I don't know what that is."

"It's a sit com. With Judd Hirsch."

"Oh! Yeah. I know that one. Got it."

"Guy used to be a comic. Now he's writing this TV show and he said he'd pass on a couple of my scripts and I went in and I met with this guy. Big deal agent. Big deal agency. He tells me he likes my scripts but that they're too esoteric. These are scripts for shows on the air now. He says, 'nobody wants to see how you can change their show. You gotta write to the formula.' And I said, 'once I've got a job, I can write to whatever they want. For samples, I want to be fully exploring the artistic possibilities within the format.'" He winced, remembering the meeting. He realized that his voice was rising, and he knew he sounded exactly as indignant, exactly as shrill as he had in that meeting.

Lindsay spoke softly, calmly, a therapist leading him through the revelation of a troubling dream. "What did he say, Daniel?"

Daniel tried to mirror her calm, but he could feel the strain in his jaw. He said, "The guy sneered at me and said, 'Artistic possibilities? Fuck artistic possibilities. It not called "show art," kid. It's called, "show business."' He tossed my scripts into my lap and he said, 'You have some talent. Now get out of my office.' And I said, 'Should I write a new spec to send you that's less interesting?' and I knew it was the wrong thing to say, but I said it anyway and he said, 'No. I'm not interested in spoon feeding you little lessons in how to make a living.'"

He returned from the window. He picked up the bong. He pulled flame through the bowl and filled his lungs with soothing smoke.

"So you keep at it. You don't let the bastards get you down. The stuff of yours that I've read, some of it matches the shows perfectly."

Daniel nodded, holding his breath. His eyes watered. He squeaked out, "Yeah. I haven't sold a goddamn thing yet and I'm already compromising the work."

"Maybe that's what you have to do for a while. But you'll find your way in. You know you will. You're too talented not to, Daniel. You know that."

Daniel shrugged. "I'm not sure talent counts for anything anymore." He set down the bong and, feeling a bit dizzy, took a knee. "I'm not proposing. I'm keeping myself from fainting."

"Yeah. I got that." She waited for him to regain his composure. She waited for him to drop into the thrift-store reading chair that did not match the couch. "You want to know why I don't have a plan? Why—Why I'm moving across the country and making a new plan?"

"Why?" Daniel asked her.

"Because I'm twenty-nine. And if you don't have a dance career going strong by the time you're thirty it's not going to happen."

"Seriously?"

"Pretty much."

"Wow."

"Yeah. You know what you don't need to be a comic? Or a television writer?"

"What?"

"Good knees. You've got time."

"I'm tired of being scared."

Lindsay nodded. "Fortunately for you, now you have your big sister moving to town to take care of you."

"Oh, good. Nothing makes me feel safer than a stoned lady with bad knees and no plan."

"Hey! Who're you calling a lady?"

Daniel chuckled.

"Mom thinks it's my own fault."

"Mom thinks what's your own fault?"

"That I didn't make it as a dancer."

"That's okay. She thinks it's Dad's fault that she didn't make it as a journalist and I'm pretty sure she thinks it's my fault that she's a terrible mother."

Lindsay laughed sharp and harsh. "Don't be ridiculous. She thinks she's a wonderful mother. She thinks it's your fault that you're an ungrateful son."

"Of course." Then, after a pause, he said, "How does she do the math?"

"What math?"

"That you're to blame for the fickle nature of a life in the arts."

Lindsay paused. "It only comes out after the second scotch, but then she gets . . ."

"Honest?"

"Scathingly honest. Both of them. They use the truth as a weapon."

Daniel nodded. "I don't think they know."

"They think they're helping."

Daniel turned the bong on the coffee table. He did not lift it. He did not reach for the lighter. "Are you going to tell me?"

"You remember Michelle?"

Daniel nodded.

"You know she . . .?" She trailed off, unable to speak the words, unwilling to find a euphemism.

Daniel nodded.

"I was really a mess. I thought I should have seen it coming. I thought I should have done something, stopped her somehow. But—it wasn't just the guilt. I also—I really loved her, you know?"

Daniel nodded. "I remember."

"I put on seven pounds."

"What?"

"I know it doesn't sound like much. But dancers . . . they want to see nothing but clean lines, elegant, long muscle. A few pounds can change the way you look, and it was just as I was starting to get in to audition for the big companies."

"Seven pounds."

"That's a lie. It was seven pounds when I auditioned for ABT. At one point, I was nine pounds over."

"Still. That's—ridiculous. But you don't believe her, do you?"

"What?"

"You know that gaining a little bit of weight for a few months doesn't mean you're at fault for—you know . . .'"

"Failing as a dancer?"

"Jesus. Linds. Seriously?"

"I'm okay. Really."

They sat in silence for a long moment. Then Daniel said, "I hate that she did that to you."

"She didn't do it to me. She just did it. She was in pain. She thought she would always be in pain. She took the only exit ramp she saw. I just got left on the highway and I was used to having someone to help navigate."

Daniel blinked, confused for a moment. Then he said, "I meant Mom."

Lindsay acknowledged the little misunderstanding with a tiny nod, the kind New Yorkers throw to one another in the hallway of an apartment building as they pass, the smallest possible upward twitch.

"You sure you're okay?"

Lindsay shrugged. "I'm making a plan."

"What've you got so far?"

"I'm eighty-four percent certain I've got an apartment to move into in a couple of days."

Daniel nodded.

"It doesn't have air conditioning, so I'll probably be over here a lot in the summer."

Daniel nodded. "This isn't an easy city to be unemployed in."

"Yeah. I'll have to figure out how to make a living. And I'll probably want to come here all the time and smoke a ton of your excellent California weed."

"Okay."

"Okay?"

"Yeah. Yeah. That sounds like a plan."

WORKS

The green room at the Laugh Works smelled so intensely of floral air freshener that Daniel found himself trying to find the under-odor that it had been sprayed to cover. He knew success would prove more troubling than curiosity, but he couldn't stop trying.

He took a moment to get his ground-legs back, listening to his breath, reminding himself that he was off stage now, that he could let go of the insistent rhythm of the four-to-one joke-per-minute pacing. He forced himself to listen to more breaths than usual this evening. He knew he had to be himself again before he lit up. He had discovered this about a year earlier. If he got high the moment he came off stage, he couldn't throw off the quick-wit for the rest of the evening. He did not know why, though he imagined someday he would do an in-depth exploration of it, figure it out. Tonight, he really wanted to get high immediately, but he wouldn't. Not until he had control of his comedic impulse.

His parents had arrived late. He had heard the whispering at the back of the room first, knew their cadences, before he saw them coming in and finding their

90

seats about eight minutes into his headlining set. He chuckled at himself and admitted that it had been closer to seven and a half minutes in, that pretending to the imprecision of 'about eight minutes' was an absurd kind of false modesty. His sense of time on stage had become supernaturally accurate. His parents had come in at seven minutes and thirty-eight seconds in, missing his opening line and a small run of jokes that ended with a punchline so off-handed in its execution that it would get a shocked laugh of surprise and delight later when he used it as a callback. It was a callback that his parents would not get because they had missed the set-up to it that was disguised as an improvised punchline.

At the moment that they had arrived he had briefly considered whether there was a way to bring them up to speed, working the punchline in again early on without it ruining the repeat-refrain for the rest of the audience. Then he'd realized that the effort was distracting him, so he let it go with a slight left-handed gesture that he realized came from resentment toward them for their late arrival.

Even as he performed, he found himself counting the number of rounds of drinks the waitress brought to their table.

They had entirely missed the terrific feature set from Barney O'Reilly.

Barney O'Reilly did a beautiful job every show. That would have been enormously helpful to him had the incompetent opener and MC, Tom Deeble not gone up after Barney and brought the room to a dead halt before doing Daniel's intro. He was quite glad that his parents had not seen Tom Deeble's set.

He sensed his readiness. He was thinking like a person again. A resentful, judgmental, slightly anxious person, but not every thought was couched in a clever turn of phrase or seen from a sardonic slant. He put on his overcoat and pulled the Marlboro pack from his pocket, the joint carefully protected between the cardboard box and the cellophane wrapping. He fished around in the deep pocket until he found the lighter and then tucked pack and lighter back into the pocket and headed out.

He passed Barney at the bar and they exchanged "great set"s with one another, pointedly ignoring Tom, who seemed not to notice. Tom flirted with the waitresses after the shows and seemed to have virtually no awareness of the others on the bill with him or the utter lack of interest shown by the women.

Daniel said, "Did you see—?"

Barney said, "They're outside. Your Dad said he wanted to smoke."

"Of course."

"He looks just like you."

"Or vice versa."

"He could be your significantly younger brother."

"Nice."

"That's as close as I come to being an insult comic."

Daniel chuckled, though he didn't mean it and stepped out into the night to find his parents. They were easy to find. Their cloud of tobacco smoke came from just upwind of the club's entrance and Daniel stepped into it.

His mother hugged him. She held him like a woman whose son had just been saved from a near drowning.

Daniel said, "Hi, Mom."

She did not let go.

Paul said, "Okay, Ellen."

She did not let go.

Over her shoulder Paul and Daniel exchanged looks of shared understanding, tolerance strained. Daniel said, "Okay, Mom."

Ellen said, "You were terrific tonight. You know that?"

"I do. Yes. Can I—?"

"You want to hug your father now?"

"Actually, I want to smoke now, but I was going hug dad first, just to be polite."

Paul said, "Aw. That's sweet. I'm touched."

Ellen let him go but she continued to stand too close, looking up at him like a girl waiting to be kissed. "When did you get so tall?"

"It's a trick of perspective. If you stand further away, I'll seem smaller."

Ellen said, "Don't be funny." She took a step back.

"No. Seriously. Much further. Until I seem to be the size that matches your memory."

Paul punched him lightly on the arm and then wrapped him in a quick hug. He whispered into Daniel's ear, the smell of scotch and smoke heavy on the words, "Really good show, Daniel. Just wonderful."

"Thanks. Is that a secret for some reason?"

Paul snorted and released his son.

Daniel pulled out the pack of cigarettes and freed the joint. "You guys don't mind, do you?"

Paul put up a hand and shook his head by way of permission.

Ellen said, "I really wish you wouldn't use that stuff."

"I know, Mom. But given the four drinks you've had this evening . . ." He let the thought hang unfinished. He thumbed the flint-wheel and the lighter clicked and sparked but did not light.

"I only had two."

"Okay." He thumbed the flint wheel for a click and a spark.

"Tell him, Paul. I almost never have more than two. That's how I know I'm not an alcoholic. I'm not one of those people who just keeps drinking."

Daniel said, "Okay."

Paul said, "Ellen."

"What?"

Daniel clicked the lighter, frustration causing him to try several times in quick succession.

"Here." Paul handed him a book of matches.

"Thanks." He lit the joint and took a long first hit. He held it in.

Paul said, "I love that smell."

"Pot? Really?"

"No. The matches. The sulfur."

"Oh. Do you want a hit?"

"Nah. I'm good."

Daniel nodded in approval.

"I got that right?"

Daniel said, "Yeah. 'nah. I'm good.' Perfect. Sounded like a bona fide prep-schooler with a half-ounce a week habit."

"Sweet."

"Wow. It's like you've been practicing."

His father wiggled his eyebrows at him and reached out with his thumb and forefinger. Daniel handed him the joint. Paul took a hit.

Ellen said, "Honestly, Paul."

"What?" but the word that started to come out of his mouth turned into a cough that came through his nose as he handed the joint back to Daniel.

Ellen said, "I didn't even finish the last one."

Paul blinked slowly. "I have no idea what we're talking about."

"There's no way I had four full rounds of scotch."

"No. You probably had three and a half. But they make them smaller than we do at home."

"Of course. That's probably it."

Daniel felt the snark rising in his chest. He felt the tension in his throat that came with joke telling back when he was in high school, when he was uncertain and couldn't know if he was funny until he heard people laugh. Rather than speaking, he listened to a single slow breath and then took a hit on the joint.

Paul said, "I'm sorry we came in so late."

"You only missed about seven and-a-half minutes of my set."

"*About* seven and a half?" Ellen's voice held a mocking tone.

"Seven minutes, thirty-eight seconds."

"You're kidding."

"You'll be able to tell when I'm kidding. There'll be humor content."

Paul snorted. Ellen dropped her cigarette to the ground, twisted the toe of her shoe on it to make sure it was fully extinguished and lit another one.

Daniel squeezed out the end of the joint, returned it to its place behind the cellophane of his cigarette pack and pulled out a Marlboro. He lit it with the matches his father had given him and then returned the pack.

Paul said, "Parking."

Daniel said, "Yeah. That can take a while."

Ellen said, "We should know better by now. We've been living in Boston for—what? Three years?"

Paul said, "Almost four. But they make them smaller here than we do at home."

Daniel laughed.

Ellen said, "I don't know what that means."

Daniel said, "It's a callback."

Paul said, "Thank you. I knew there was a name for it."

"You two!" and Paul and Daniel exchanged a look, both knowing that her playful scolding tone covered a lack of comprehension.

They stood in silence for a bit, smoking.

Paul said, "There was one thing you said that got a laugh that I—"

Daniel said, "Exactly."

Paul nodded.

Ellen said, "Okay. Now you're doing it on purpose."

"You remember when everyone laughed and you leaned over and said, 'why is that funny?'"

"Yes! I do. I wanted to ask about that."

Daniel said, "It's a callback to a joke I do in the first five minutes, so you guys didn't get it."

Ellen said, "And that makes it funny?"

Daniel said, "Yes."

"Well, I still don't really get it, I guess."

"Yeah. Because . . . never mind. Just trust me. It's funny."

Paul sighed.

Ellen raised her fingers in a gesture that was intended to be a light indication that she was throwing her hands up in the air but only looked as though she was tickling a cow's underbelly. "I don't really understand how a lot of it works."

"You don't need to."

"But I really am so glad we got to come see you while you're in town."

"Yeah. Yeah. Me too."

Paul said, "And you're doing this show all weekend?"

"Yeah."

"And . . . how much of it is—you know—ad libbed or whatever?"

"Very little. Sometimes more. Usually less."

"It's very impressive."

"Thank you. I live to impress."

"I know that about you."

Daniel nodded.

"It makes me fear I have failed as a parent."

"You have."

Paul chuckled. "Ah, the joy of living without subtext."

"Yeah. That's what's going on here."

Ellen said, "There is one thing I wanted to tell you."

Paul winced. Daniel saw it and recognized it as the exact expression he had repressed, not being four rounds into transparency.

"When you went after that guy who talked to you . . ."

"Yes."

"You did that whole thing about, 'I am much cooler than you are!'"

"'You can't outcool me.'"

"What?"

"The heckler response. It's not, 'I am much cooler than you are!' It's, 'You can't outcool me.'"

"I don't get the difference."

"Nuance and . . . craft. Go ahead."

"Well, I know the people were all laughing and everything when you did the list but then –"

"Yeah. Sorry about that."

"You don't know what I'm going to say."

"Ellen," Paul warned, almost begging.

"What is that list you did? How did that go? Do you remember?"

"Yes. I remember the bit."

"That's a bit?"

"Yes."

"So . . . do you—what? Do you tell someone in the audience to yell at you so you can do that bit?"

"What? No."

"Ellen."

"What? I don't know how it all works."

Daniel stopped himself from sighing. He spoke from the top of his breath, lungs full, expelling none of his power before he began. "That's my go-to heckler response. If someone heckles me, I do that bit. I have a couple of others of increasing intensity and hostility because I hate hecklers. The list is, 'You can't outcool me. I have a microphone and a spotlight. You can't outcool me. I get my drugs delivered. You can't outcool me. In 1958 my father slept with Allen Ginsberg. You can't outcool me.'"

Ellen pursed her lips.

"And you were going to say that you wish I wouldn't say that Dad slept with Allen Ginsberg."

"Well, I just don't think it's very funny."

"And yet, you heard the laugh it gets."

"Well, I think that's just because—you know . . ."

Paul said, "I don't think that's right." His thoughtful tone suggested that he might launch into a full hermeneutic examination of the nature of that joke and the laugh it elicited.

"No?"

"No. That's not just a homophobia trigger. It's also a particularly erudite social reference. I think different people in the audience are laughing at it for all sorts of different reasons. It says interesting things about the performer and his relationship to his father, his own social class, his upbringing, his education, how comfortable *he* is with homosexuality. It's a complicated joke, really."

Daniel said, "Thank you. Also . . . it's true. Isn't it?"

Ellen said, "It makes me very uncomfortable."

"Well, you're not usually there, so . . ."

Paul said, "I never slept with Allen Ginsberg."

Ellen said, "What?"

"You thought I slept with Allen?"

She pursed her lips.

Daniel said, "I always thought you slept with Allen Ginsberg."

"Why did you think that?"

Daniel took a drag from his cigarette, thinking. He said, "I'm not sure. Something about the way Mom responds whenever his name comes up, I think."

"I knew him. You know, when we lived in San Francisco. But no. We never slept together."

Ellen's words came out a little bit rough and in a cloud of cigarette smoke. "Well, you certainly liked spending time with him and . . . those other boys."

"Yes. Yes, I did. But Allen? No. We never—you thought I slept with Allen?"

Ellen blinked, rearranging memories from long ago. "Maybe we should discuss this when we're all sober."

Daniel said, "When would that be, exactly?"

"Daniel. Don't be funny."

Paul said to him, sharply, almost angrily, "Be kinder, Daniel. Try." After a tiny pause he said softly, "Your mother has more to repress than you can imagine."

"Wait a minute. Wait a minute. Wait a minute. Does it bother you less if you know it's not true?"

Ellen said, "I don't know. I don't—all these years I thought that was your big secret."

Paul snorted. He squeezed his nose. "What makes you think there's only one?"

"Now don't *you* start with the jokes."

Paul stepped behind her and wrapped his arms around her. She held his arms against her chest as he rested his chin on her shoulder.

Daniel took a step back, just enough to bring them into a different focus as a couple. He could see fragments of youth in their spooned embrace. He could see time and shared history, a comfort in one another's shape that could only come from decades of familiarity. "Sometimes, I think the secrets we worry about don't matter nearly as much as the things we all know about one another."

Paul raised his eyebrows, surprised, running the sentence over again in his head.

Ellen tilted her head to side so that her temple pressed to her husband's cheek.

Paul said, "What time do you fly out on Sunday? Maybe we could all meet up for a brunch somewhere."

"I could do that. That'd be nice." The words surprised Daniel as he spoke them. He wondered if he'd smoked more of that joint than he'd realized.

Ellen said, "Oooh! Can we meet at the DuMarnez?"

Paul said, "What a good idea. Let's do that."

Daniel, not knowing what that was, said, "Okay. I'll get directions at the hotel."

Ellen said, "I don't usually drink during the day. I mean, you know, not until later on. But they have the most wonderful Bloody Maries there.

"Ah."

Paul said, "They also have, you know. Food."

"Of course. Right. Good. So. Sunday. At eleven?"

Paul said, "Great. Okay. So . . ."

"Should I get you guys a cab?"

Paul waved him off with a gesture that meant 'I'm fine to drive,' and Daniel believed him because it was easier than taking responsibility for their risky behavior.

Ellen peeled herself free of her husband's arms and wrapped herself around Daniel for just a moment. She said, "I think you really might be finally growing up into a genuinely decent person. You know that?"

"Okay. I love you, too, Mom."

"And thank you for promising not to do that bit anymore."

Daniel glanced at his father who gave him a gesture that said, 'It doesn't matter. Let it go.' So, Daniel did not correct her.

Paul wrapped him in a quick hug and patted his back. "Okay, Buddy. I'll see you Sunday."

They turned away and wrapped arms around one another. Daniel watched them move off down the sidewalk, remarkably steady for the amount they'd drunk. He watched the easy gait of their affection, a loving couple, perhaps on the way to the school bus after band practice or off to the library after an English Lit lecture, their lives spiraling out behind them, intertwined, tangled, but still flowing like joyous ribbons. He wondered how he had never seen it before.

He shouted, "Hey, Mom?"

His parents turned to look at him from all the way down near the corner. He shouted, "Am I about the right size now?"

"Perfect, Honey! This is how I remember you."

Paul shouted, "Come by the apartment after Brunch. We'll stand you up in a doorway and do a pencil mark."

Daniel snorted. He squeezed his nose.

His parents walked away. He pulled the joint from the cigarette wrapper and realized his lighter didn't work. He put the joint away and watched them go, shrinking into the distance.

He wondered why it is so much easier to like people when they are very, very small.

UNSPOKEN

Paul set out the scrabble board as he did every afternoon. Ellen shook the bag with the lettered tiles, the familiar rattling sound a source of comfort. They each picked an initial letter to find out who got to pull tiles and play first. They did not need to speak during this process. Whoever pulled the letter that came earlier alphabetically would choose and play first. The other person would pour drinks. It was so much a part of the game it might as well have been printed as part of the instructions inside the lid of the box.

They showed one another their single tiles and Paul went to pour. Ellen was secretly glad, not because she liked to go first but because Paul poured more generously. She always tried to keep each drink close to an actual shot's worth although she did it by eye rather than measuring. Paul showed less concern for appearances. Ellen didn't really know why she cared so much when it was just the two of them. She did though. She tried to keep each drink down to two fingers at the most.

He brought the ice-clinking glasses back with him as she arranged the tiles on her little plastic rack. She sipped her drink and said, "Jameson?"

"Yeah. Sorry. Did you want the MacAllen?"

"No. This is good. This is nice."

She put out tiles. She counted points. She marked the number on a score sheet made from the back of a letter folded down the center to create a long, thin strip.

She did not say that Daniel had called her during the day. She sipped her Irish Whiskey and pulled replacement tiles from the bag.

Paul examined his tiles. He looked at the letters on the board. He looked at the letters on his rack. He rearranged them on the rack, anagramming. He did not say that he had seen the envelope addressed to their son, stamped, waiting near the outgoing mail. He had not lifted it to the light to see through to the contents. He knew what it was. He didn't know how much it was made out for, but that really wasn't the issue.

He played his first word parallel to hers, overlapping and extending beyond it, dragging double points from the first three letters he played plus points from her letters.

She counted the points, marked them on the score sheet and examined the layout of the board. "We're starting with that are we?"

Paul snorted acknowledgement. He sipped his Irish. He pulled new tiles from the bag. He did not ask her how much she was sending to Daniel. He did not ask whether it was more or less than the young man had requested.

Ellen put out a simple word, short and low-scoring, but it allowed her to get some of the vowels off her rack. She hated the silence. She hated having secrets hanging in the room. She didn't know why she kept it a secret, really. It wasn't as if Paul would ever forbid her to send Daniel money. That wasn't how they functioned as a couple. He would just be annoyed. Exactly that. He would be annoyed in the passive voice. He would get scoldy or, worse, just clench his jaw so that she could see the muscles working at the side of his face as he held back the quiet, judgmental irritation. Still, the secrecy didn't make any real sense. He would know eventually if he didn't know already. He always seemed to know already when she told him. Every time.

Paul placed another word on the board, managing now to both parallel and intersect, milking double and triple impact from every bit of each word, the primary and the incidental. He made them count, the words he made. He got extra value wherever he could.

He drained his glass and stood up to refill it. A glance at Ellen's led her to check it. She paused to imply that it was a considered decision and then held hers up to him for refilling.

Through all of this, NPR droned through the old component audio system. Neither of them listened to the reports, the stories of partisan wrangling and rumors of executive level misconduct. Today, Paul and Ellen let the soothing sounds of informative journalism slide past as a minimalist, monotone movie score under the silencescape of their afternoon.

Paul returned with the drinks.

Ellen sipped. She studied her letters. She rearranged them, almost certain a seven-letter big score hid in there somewhere.

Paul took a long pull on his drink. He lit a cigarette with a plastic, disposable lighter. For the five-thousandth time he said, "I sort of miss that whiff of sulfer."

"I know, honey. Nothing's what it was."

He had enough of the Irish in him now. He said, "How much this time?"

Ellen winced. She held up a finger to silence him while she placed her tiles on the board, counting points, adding them to her score. Only after she had counted seven new tiles from the bag did she say, "Twenty-five."

"Twenty-five hundred?"

She nodded.

"Jesus."

He placed his single word, over-weighted on the board and Ellen tallied his score. Even with her big-word bonus he was within five points of her. "He fell behind on rent."

"He always seems to have enough for grass." He sipped his drink.

"Can we not do this?"

"You know you're enabling him. You know that, right?"

"The economy isn't what it was when we were their age."

Then the silence fell again for a bit. She played a word. He played a word. Someone on NPR talked to a factory worker who did not understand international markets about how he would be affected by changes in international markets.

"Some birds will just sit in the nest unless the mothers push them out to fall or fly."

Ellen said, "I don't think that's right."

"No. It's true."

"Well I'm not that kind of bird."

The pause was long and filled with sipping and playing. "Maybe *he* is that kind of bird."

"You want me to tear up the check? I can call him and tell him it's not coming."

"Don't make me the bad guy here."

"That's not—I didn't mean to be doing that."

They placed tiles. They clinked ice.

"How much time did he spend telling you how well things were going before he asked?"

"A lot." Then, after just a tiny beat, "How did we do it so wrong?"

"I don't know that we did."

"I'm not a terrible mother, am I?"

Paul shrugged. "There's no manual. There's no right way." After his own tiny beat, he conceded, "It might've been me. I don't know. I don't know anything."

Ellen did her final addition. She showed the sheet to Paul.

"Good game. Another?"

Ellen handed him her glass. She folded the gameboard up the middle, jumbling all the tiles and using it to channel the tiles back, all the words broken up and returned to the bag.

She shook the bag less to mix the letters, she realized, than because she found the sound so comforting.

LAYOVER (TWO)

"We've got to stop meeting like this." Paul wrapped Daniel in a hug, oblivious to the woman who very nearly tripped over his rolling carry-on.

"Welcome back to the homeland. How was the flight?"

"Long." He disengaged from the hug, grabbed the handle of the luggage and steered it toward a table. "It's good to have my feet back on the ground."

"They checked your real luggage all the way through?"

"Yeah. It'll meet me in Boston."

Daniel nodded.

Paul dropped the strap of his shoulder bag over the extension handle on his rolling case. "You want anything? I'm having scotch."

"No. I'm okay."

"Right. You have to drive."

"Yes."

"Everyone always has to drive in Los Angeles. I don't know why they even stock alcohol."

"It's in case you and Mom come to visit."

"That's less funny than you imagine."

"You know what? Get me a coffee."

"Okay." Paul abandoned Daniel, heading for the bar.

Daniel watched him take the few steps, the ever-present limp more pronounced with the effects of the long flight and his father's age. Paul looked smaller than Daniel remembered, thinner.

After a moment of conversation with the bartender, Paul returned empty handed. "They'll bring it over."

"Okay."

"I got the sense that he was annoyed with me for not waiting for the waitress."

"Okay."

"They spoiled me in India."

"Treated you well, did they?"

"Incredibly accommodating. I felt like a star, I tell you! A star!" He raised his hand in a gesture that was intended to seem grand and self-mocking but actually had the look of a man awkwardly screwing in a light bulb.

"Well, there's nothing like an airport server to ground a person."

Paul snorted. "It looks like they're going to bring me back next year for significantly longer."

"Cool."

"There's an arts council in Mumbai. They think I can be helpful in putting together a long-term strategy for curation and scheduling."

"That sounds . . . sort of up your alley."

"They don't say scheduling. They kept saying, 'calendaring.' It was so hard not to correct them every time."

"I can only imagine."

"I hate it when people verb their nouns."

"That's funny."

"I don't think it's mine."

"Okay."

"I mean, you probably shouldn't use it."

"I wasn't going to."

"I think it's from Danny Simon."

"Neil Simon's brother, Danny Simon?"

"Yes."

"Do you know him?"

"No."

"Okay."

A waitress brought Paul's scotch and put it on a small paper napkin. She put a cup of coffee in front of Daniel with a small bowl filled with small plastic half-and-half containers.

Daniel picked one up. He read the label aloud. "Oooh. Half-and-half-and-half. Now with fifty percent more!"

Paul said, "That's funny."

"Yeah. It's not mine."

Paul said, "Okay. I wasn't going to use it."

Daniel said, "I got it from Opus Moreschi."

"I don't know who that is."

"He's the Danny Simon of today."

"So, he's Bruce Villanche's brother?"

Daniel chuckled. "No. That would still be the Danny Simon of Yesterday."

"I thought Danny Simon was the Danny Simon of Yesterday."

"Danny Simon is the Danny Simon of two Thursdays ago at least."

"So, you came to meet me at the airport just to remind me that I'm old?"

"I'm not the one who started in with shtick from

Danny Simon."

Paul chuckled. He sipped his scotch. He spun the little stir stick then tapped it on the edge of the glass and set it on the napkin. He lined it up carefully, parallel with the edge of the napkin and then pushed the overhanging end with his thumb so that it lay flush. "Lindsay couldn't make it, huh?"

"She said she has a meeting."

"Who has meetings this late in the day?"

"People who are well connected enough to get meetings but not important enough to get drive-on passes."

"I don't understand this city."

"I know." Then, after a short pause, he looked into his coffee cup and said to the beverage, "I'm not sure I do either."

Paul became suddenly interested. "What's that about?"

Daniel shrugged. "I just booked another little mini-tour. Comedy Stop at the Trop in Vegas, then up to Reno, Park City and Salt Lake City in Utah, then across to Redding and back down the coast with stops in San Francisco, San Luis Obispo, Santa Barbara . . . and then I'm back home."

"That sounds good."

"It feels like I'm going in circles."

"I thought this was the life you wanted."

"Nobody moves to Los Angeles because they want to be on the road. I thought I'd be rich and famous by now."

"Is that what you want?"

"It really, really is."

Paul shook his head sadly.

Daniel sipped his coffee. He let his stir stick drip onto

a napkin and then stood it on end, holding it upright with the pressure of a fingertip on its top.

"What does this have to do with your sister?"

"What?"

"Who is Lindsay meeting with?"

"It doesn't matter. She's doing great. Thriving. I'm proud of her. Really."

"I thought she was living in a crappy apartment and coming to yours when she needed air conditioning."

"Yeah. She's looking for a new place now."

"Oh. I don't think I knew that."

"She placed a script. You know that, right?"

"She called your mother while I was overseas and then e-mailed me. She got into the Guild, she said."

"Yeah."

"But you're touring. You're getting bookings."

"I don't need more bookings. I mean—of course I need more bookings. But I need the meetings. I need to—I don't know—I need to get invited to the right parties."

"I don't understand this city."

"Yeah. You said."

"You know how young you are, don't you?"

Daniel shrugged. "It doesn't much matter how much time I've got, if I spend it all running in circles."

"Lindsay said you helped her a lot with her first script."

"Yeah. But she's doing what she's doing on her own. She's—she runs in the right circles."

Paul turned his glass slowly on the napkin, careful not to disturb the placement of his stir stick. "This city is saturated in desperation."

"Yes. Desperation and fear."

"Huh. What are you afraid of?"

Daniel thought about it for a moment. He winced, hating his answer. "I'm afraid of becoming the Danny Simon of tomorrow."

"He's had a long, respected and storied career."

"Yes. As Neil Simon's brother."

COMEDY OF MANNERS

Ellen sipped her scotch. Paul turned his wine glass slowly on the paper cocktail napkin, spreading a spilled drop into a red circle.

"I don't know why we couldn't have chosen some place nicer," Ellen said.

"She said she wanted to buy us dinner," Paul said. "I was trying to be polite."

"Still. We could have gone somewhere decent and then insisted on picking up the bill."

"This is decent."

"You know what I mean."

"You mean you prefer the eighteen-year-old Macallan to the twelve."

Ellen gave him the look that meant, you're not at all funny, and then said, "this is Dewars." Then, responding to his apologetic shrug, "They have twelve and eighteen. But if she's buying . . ."

"We really are very decent, polite people." He sipped his wine.

"Is she late?"

"We're early."

"I should've gotten the Macallan and paid for it separately."

"You still can."

"Too late." She didn't quite nod toward the front of the restaurant and Paul turned to see Lindsay out there on the sidewalk, beyond the glass, moving toward the door. He read the body language as best he could, but there wasn't much to go on and he could never tell the difference between chilly and irritable anyway. Or needing to pee.

In hushed tones, a hurried whisper, Ellen said, "Don't push her about grad school." Lindsay came toward them and then Paul was up, out of his seat to watch her approach.

He took in her coat, slouchy soft in a way that suggested it had been expensive originally. He imagined her, out there in Los Angeles, going through the racks at thrift stores, keeping up appearances. She looked thin, too. Fit. He opened his arms and she hugged him affectionately, smelling of shampoo and autumn.

Ellen remained seated so that Lindsay had to lean over her shoulder to kiss her, and Ellen returned the kiss awkwardly, patted a conveniently placed hand and gestured for one of the empty seats at the four-top.

Lindsay said, "Actually, can we—?" She turned to a passing waiter, "Can we move to that booth in the back? Is that going to mess things up for you guys?"

"That's fine. Let me just—" He looked at Lindsay, saw something in her demeanor that altered his tone and said, "I'll let your server know." He hurried off as though he'd been sent on a very important errand. Ellen stood up and collected her drink.

Paul lifted his coat from the back of the chair where

he'd draped it, grabbed Ellen's coat as well. "Would you grab my wine, Baby Girl?"

"It's okay, Dad. They'll bring it over."

"I don't like to make extra work for them. Would you?"

Lindsay sighed a sigh that held in it a lifetime of tiny battles lost, tiny points conceded. She picked up the wine. She also picked up the circle-stained cocktail napkin to avoid that additional moment of dialogue. Ellen was already on her way to the back booth with a forced cheer in her gait to indicate a false lack of irritation at the displacement. Lindsay and Paul followed.

They settled in.

"So," Paul said as an opening probe, "You're in town."

"Yes. Just for a couple of nights."

"Working."

"Yes."

"Is this a television thing?" Ellen asked. "Or one of those other things?"

"What other things?"

"Sometimes you do those other—what do you call them? You know what I'm talking about, Paul. Borging or something."

"Blogging?" Lindsay asked.

"Right! Those."

"I was a blogger for three years, Mom. For a travel site. I know you read at least some of the posts."

"I did read some of them. You know. On the computer. When you sent me the things to click on."

Paul winced.

"The links?"

"Right! The links to the blogging! All the new language. It really is something. Anyway, I only read them on the computer. You know. Where you scroll through and read all the text and see the pictures and it's all just on one long page."

"As opposed to what, Mom?"

"Well, you know, I didn't go out and try to find copies of the—you know—the actual thing."

"Ellen."

"What?"

Lindsay said, "What actual thing?"

"You know. The magazine or the little booklet or wherever they were really publishing the stuff."

"What?"

"Oh, come on, now. Don't be like that. I read all the ones you sent me the clicky things to."

Paul said, "Links."

"Right! Sometimes I even left comments."

"Yes."

"Right there at the bottom. Did you read those?"

"Yes."

"I remember once I typed, 'This was really well written! Thanks for sending it!' and sometimes if there were little mistakes with punctuation or grammar, I pointed it out for you."

"Yes. I remember."

"'Cause, you know, I figure if I can help in any way."

"Yes."

Paul said, "You did that in the comments section?"

"Sure! That way she could fix it, maybe, before it actually got published or printed or whatever."

"Ellen."

"What?"

"I'm not doing that any more. I'm here with a location

shoot."

Ellen said, "Isn't that wonderful."

A waitress approached the table. She introduced herself. "Hi. I'm Signe. I'll be your server this evening."

Ellen said, "You already told us that."

"Yes. But I was introducing myself to the other young lady."

"Hello, Signe. I'm Lindsay."

"She doesn't need to know that, Honey," Paul said.

Ellen pulled down the last of her scotch and then crunched a bit of ice in her teeth as she slid the glass toward the waitress.

Signe did not respond to that. "Can I bring you anything to drink? Have you had a chance to look at the menu?"

"I haven't. I'm sorry. Do you have any herbal tea?"

Signe listed some teas and Lindsay chose one. Then Signe turned to Ellen. "Would you like another Dewar's?"

"Please."

"Not Macallan?" Lindsay asked.

"Oh, that's not necessary."

"Bring her a glass of your oldest Macallan and if the bartender grumbles about putting it on the rocks tell him that when he can afford good scotch he can decide how he wants it served."

Signe said to Ellen, "We have a twenty-five-year-old."

"Oh, that's just absurd. Eighteen is fine."

"Okay."

Lindsay said, "Bring the twenty-five."

Signe left them alone.

"So, you're shooting a location?" Ellen said.

"We're shooting on location. Have you seen the

show?"

"What show, Honey?"

Lindsay blinked slowly. "I told you about this. In an e-mail. Last year."

"About what, Dear? You know I don't understand half of what you say when you're talking about work." Ellen patted her daughter's hand.

Paul waved to Signe as she approached with the fresh scotch and pointed at his empty wine glass.

"*Served Cold*. TNT? Thursday nights?"

Ellen said, "Oh! I heard about that show. You remember, Paul?"

"What are we talking about now?"

"That show! The one Stacy Kiel was going on about the other night. And on NPR . . . what's his name? Oh, help me out here, Paul. The guy with the funny inflection."

"Bander Sujianmati."

"Yes! That's the one. He did a whole piece on it, about how it's so violent and angry . . ."

"Oh!" Paul suddenly said, engaged. "I remember that review. He compared it to the whole Quentin Tarentino thing in cinema and talked about how it all started with Kubrick's *The Shining*. The—I loved this line—'the celebration of our darkest impulses; the repeated affirmation of an underlying hostility, a fundamental violence at the heart of every family.'"

"Yes! I don't know how you remember whole chunks like that."

"It struck me when I heard it. I remember."

"It stars that woman, I think. The one who used to be on that other show. The comedy. We never watched that either. Except that one episode you wrote. You remember that, Honey? You called us all excited 'cause you'd sold one episode to this ridiculous sit com on network television?"

"Show Me the Love," Lindsay informed her. "Yes. I remember."

Paul said, "You were so excited to be getting into the Guild."

"Yes."

Ellen said, "And then we tried to watch it and we just couldn't even sit through the whole half hour, it was such utter schlock. I mean, I'm sure you did a wonderful job of writing just what they wanted but it was all those corny one-liners and then the big fake laughs from the studio audience. Just ridiculous."

"Okay."

Paul said, "But you were so excited about selling that episode and getting into the Guild. I remember that. What was that? Three years ago? Four?"

Signe put Paul's full glass of wine on a fresh new cocktail napkin. She put a small tin of steeping tea beside a tea cup for Lindsay. She paused for a moment, then said, "I'll be back in just a minute to take your orders. Okay?"

Paul waved her away without looking.

Lindsay said, "Thank you, Signe."

Lindsay's phone made a small noise. She ignored it. "So. What have you guys been up to? Dad, you have to be starting to think about retirement."

"I don't want to talk about it."

"And yet, he does. Several times a day. Usually half a sentence grumbled into the refrigerator."

Paul sipped his wine. He crinkled his eyes in the way that told both Lindsay and Ellen that he was about to say something but wasn't sure how it would be received.

"Lindsay, I want to say something."

"I'm not going to graduate school."

"That's not what I was going to say." But then he didn't go on at all.

Lindsay poured tea into her cup. She waited. She sipped.

Ellen said, "You're not drinking at all now?"

"I have an early call tomorrow morning."

"To whom?"

"What?"

"Who do you have to call early tomorrow?"

"That's—no. That's what time I have to get to work. It's called a call time."

"Oh."

Paul said, "We don't really know all the lingo."

"I know."

Abruptly, Paul blurted out, in an oddly scolding tone, "You know we love you, right?"

"I do. Sometimes I wish you could love me with, you know, less hostility."

Paul chuckled. "I get that."

Ellen said, "I still drink."

"Yes. I see that."

Ellen said, "Your father really only drinks wine, but I just love scotch. Mostly only in the evenings."

"Mostly?"

"Sometimes on the weekend, if we're playing Scrabble, you know, and it's the afternoon."

"Ah."

"Ellen."

Ellen said, as though she was answering a question that nobody had asked, "Never more than two."

"Okay."

Ellen said, "I know my limit. That's how I know I'm not an alcoholic. Just two drinks and no more. If I have too much I fall down. Literally. One time I went to sit on the toilet and woke up on the floor of the bathroom."

Paul said, "Good story."

Lindsay said, "And this is how you know you're not an alcoholic?"

"Don't be like that." Ellen stood up. "You know what I want, right, Paul? You can order for us. I'm going out to have a cigarette while we wait for the food."

She made her way to the front door.

Lindsay and Paul sat in silence for a moment.

"We're missing something, aren't we?"

Lindsay nodded. "It doesn't matter, Dad."

He said, "I don't know what you want from us."

She shrugged. "It'd be nice if you said you were proud of me."

"Oh, Honey. We are so, so proud of you. We tell people all the time about how wonderfully you turned out. We might have made some mistakes as parents, but you are proof that we were not completely incompetent."

Lindsay chuckled. "Is that what I am?"

"What?"

"Proof of your competence."

"I don't understand."

They sat in silence for a moment. Her phone made a noise. She reached into her purse and fished it out. She swiped through the combination to bring her screen to life. She began scrolling through texts.

Paul said, "Don't do that."

"What?"

"Look at your phone in the middle of a conversation."

"It was actually the middle of a pause."

"Still."

"It's not five o'clock yet in L.A. I'm still working, Dad."

"You're at a restaurant. With your parents."

"One of them."

"It's rude. Put it away."

"Rude? Your wife just walked out of the room to have a cigarette. I waited until there was a pause, and now I'm checking through a great many texts, some of which I really should have responded to when they came in."

"Really? You're so important that people in L.A. need you to get back to them right away when they text you in Boston?"

"I'm not on vacation, Dad. Yes. They need me to get back to them."

"Oh, stop it. You're just avoiding talking to me."

"Now who's overestimating their importance?"

"What?"

She finished thumbing out a response to the texts and put the phone back into her purse.

Ellen returned in a small cloud of eau de Parliament. "What'd I miss?"

"We had a fight."

"Oooh. Exciting. What about? Did you offer to pay for grad school?"

"I told her it was rude to look at her phone at the dinner table."

"Oh! Your father is right about that dear. I read about it in the advice column in the paper. It's not Dear Abby. I don't remember her name. But someone wrote in about that and she said that it's very rude. Very common now, but totally unacceptable."

"Is that what you read about it in your print-medium newspaper, Mom?" She heard the defensive anger in her own voice.

"What does that mean?"

Lindsay sighed.

"Wait. I remembered something when I was outside. You started saying something and then we got sidetracked. Something about that awful show on the Dynamite Channel."

"TNT. Not the Dynamite Channel."

"I know, dear. I like to call it the Dynamite Channel."

Lindsay waved to Signe who came at once. "Are you all ready to order?"

Paul said, "My wife and I would like to split a Cobb Salad. Is that allowed?"

"Of course. Do you want that all chopped up and mixed to make things easy or—"

"Oh, do it the way you usually do it. I like when it's all fancy in the separate wedges and then I get to mix it up myself," Ellen said.

"Okay. And for you?"

"You know what? Do you still have the bisque?"

"I love the bisque. Would you like a cup or—"

"A bowl."

"Terrific," Signe jotted it on her pad.

"A big bowl. Does it come in extra-large? Do you have a tureen of bisque that I could order?"

Signe laughed. "One venti bisque. If the bowl's not enough for you, I'll bring you a second one and only charge you exactly the same amount for that one."

"Wow. You made that sound like a bargain. You're

awesome."

"I strive to not suck." Signe smiled as she collected the menus.

Ellen finished off her drink and handed Signe the glass. "Could I have another of those?"

"Of course."

Signe went.

Ellen seemed to respond to an accusation. "Oh, come on. The first one was just Dewar's."

"Ellen."

Ellen turned to Lindsay, "I wish you wouldn't do that."

"What do you wish I wouldn't do?"

"Make jokes with waitresses like that."

"What kind of waitresses should I make jokes with?"

"You know what I mean. Stop being funny. Everyone finds it exhausting."

Lindsay closed her eyes in a way that suggested that she had a terrible headache, although she did not. She opened them again and sipped her tea.

Paul said, "So, is that what you're working on?"

"What?"

"That TNT show? Cold Servings?"

"*Served Cold.*"

"Yes."

"Oh. I didn't realize you worked on that show." Ellen tapped the tips of each of her fingers with her thumb nervously.

"I know. I got that."

"What do you do on it?"

"It doesn't matter. Just . . . let's eat and talk about something else."

"Are you upset because I said what I heard on NPR?

That wasn't my opinion. I've never even watched the thing."

"Yeah. Got that."

Signe set down a fresh drink for Ellen. Paul sipped his wine.

"Are you upset because we never watch it?"

"A little. Yes."

"Because you work on it? I didn't realize you worked on it, Honey." Ellen's inflection implied that she believed her words were an apology.

"I sent you an e-mail when it went to pilot. Another when it was picked up."

"I know, Honey. But I don't really know what all of that means."

"So," Paul said, "You've really been with this thing from the beginning."

"Yes. The very beginning."

"I can see how that feels important to you, Baby Girl. But it's still just a TV show."

"No. It's not, Dad. It's not just a TV show. It's my show. It's my series. We're out here shooting a bunch of location scenes for the second season. We're picked up for a second season. My show."

Ellen said, "Oh, don't be pretentious about it. So you work on a show. It doesn't make it yours."

"I'm not—it is my show."

Paul corrected her as gently as he could. "No. It's that woman's, from that other show. The comedy."

"She's the star, Dad. I created it. I Executive Produce it. It's my show."

Signe brought the salad and the bisque. She put down an extra plate so that Ellen and Paul could split the salad.

Ellen set about mixing the salad together. "I love this part!"

As Paul moved some of the newly mixed salad to the extra plate, Ellen sipped her scotch.

Paul said, "We don't really know what any of that means."

"I pitched a show. Then I wrote the pilot. Then I sold the show. Then we made twenty-two episodes of which I wrote nine while overseeing the writing staff that wrote the others."

Ellen forked lettuce with a fork. "Well, I think it's great that you're working, but I don't think that's the kind of thing you should be bragging about. I mean, don't put this Cold Justice thing on your resume."

"*Served Cold.*"

"Whatever it's called."

"Ellen." He said it while looking at his daughter. Then, "This is the thing, isn't it? The thing we were missing?"

Lindsay nodded.

"You're—that's a big deal, selling and running a show."

Lindsay nodded.

"I don't even see how you would know how to do all of that."

"Ellen."

"It doesn't matter, Mom." She blew on a spoonful of bisque.

"Seriously, though, Honey, I think it's great that you're making a living doing this TV stuff while you're working on your real writing and whatever, but you shouldn't tell people you're working on that awful show."

Paul sighed.

"Why's that, Mom?"

"Because nobody likes it. Apparently, it's very violent."

"It's consistently beating out the big three networks in its time slot."

"That doesn't mean anybody likes it."

"Actually, Mom, it means a lot of people like it."

"Well, that doesn't mean it's any good. A lot of people thought Milton Berle was funnier than Jack Benny. A lot of people liked the Stooges more than the Marx Brothers."

"Okay, Mom."

"I hope you're socking away a lot of money in the bank so that you have something of a cushion, and you can just relax when that show is over and do your real writing."

"This is real writing."

"It's television," Paul said.

"It's been called innovative television. And—we're getting terrific ratings. And we got picked up for a second season." She heard her voice getting higher. She heard the plea behind it, the need to be heard, to be recognized.

Her father said, "Well, I suppose that's the sort of thing people in L.A. would be very impressed by." Then, after the shortest of beats, "I don't know what you think you need my approval for."

Lindsay sighed. She pulled bisque into her mouth, focusing on the sound and then sensation of the warm broth.

Paul said, "Don't slurp, Baby Girl. It's very rude."

"It really is," Ellen said. She signaled the waitress that her glass was empty.

HUNGER

Tessa assured Daniel that Lindsay would be just another minute or two, that she was wrapping up a call. She asked if he was sure he didn't want coffee or water. He assured her that he was fine. She left him alone.

He pulled his Blackberry from his pocket and worked the trackball with his thumb, scrolling through e-mail subject lines absently, hoping the list would refresh to show him something new, something interesting. He put the phone away.

He studied the poster framed behind glass on the wall opposite him, the icicles that took on the look of gun barrels pointing downward from the eaves of a suburban house, the family standing together on the steps forcing smiles. He noticed for the first time that the frozen puddles along the walkway that led to the house doubled as bullet holes, that the reflected sunset played as subliminal blood-streaks. He wondered how much of that had been at Lindsay's direction and how much had been the independent work of an art department.

From beyond the upholstered wall that separated him from the office proper three different voices reached him, answering phones. One of them, of course, was Tess. A chirping phone would stop abruptly, and she would say, "Lindsay Grunman's office. This is Tess." One of them he knew to be the young black man he had seen walking through a few minutes earlier with a freshly refilled coffee mug emblazoned with the logo-title of *Served Cold*, the show Daniel's sister had created and now executive produced. When he answered the phone, it was with a slightly mumbled, "Family Dynamic. How should I direct your call?" The third voice was a female whom Daniel had not yet seen. She answered, "This is Claudia!" her inflection somehow implying that she was quite certain her number had been dialed by mistake. While Tessa generally informed people that "She's on with the network and will have to return," and the young man who served as general reception for the production company almost never said anything beyond, "how should I direct your call?" Claudia provided answers to questions that Daniel could begin to guess at based on the part of the conversations that he could hear. She said things like, "The music cues for that are already on the wiki. If you can't find the file by ep number, try by date," or, "No, it needs to be a full bottle show. The whole thing, she said. Blowing up the boat in ep 4 leaves us way too tight for locations that week."

After a while, Daniel went around the upholstered wall and said, "You know what, Tess? Tell her I'll call her tomorrow. We can talk by phone."

"Oh! No. Don't go. I know she was looking forward to—"

"We were scheduled for one-thirty."

"She's just running a little bit behind. I'm sure she'll be

off soon."

"I have other things scheduled this afternoon," Daniel lied.

"I don't know if you understand how busy –"

From beyond the closed door just beyond Tess's desk-cubby, Lindsay shouted, "Just bring him in, Tess. I'll deal with him."

Tess shrugged a 'you see?' at Daniel and opened Lindsay's door, allowing him to go in. She hovered in the door as he stood awkwardly for a moment. Lindsay held up a finger as she said into her Bluetooth, "I think it's a great idea. Dark is good. Dark is real." She listened to the voice that Daniel could not hear and moved her hand like the mouth of a puppet, telling him that the person at the other end was talking and talking and talking and boring.

Daniel chuckled.

"Look, I think I've got the gist of this and I can make sure we start to seed the season three sub-plot as we script these last four episodes for this year. I've got someone in my office who's been waiting and I'm starting to feel like I'm being rude." She closed her eyes for a moment and rocked her head back and forth, listening to meaningless sign-off chatter. "Okay. You too. Talk Tuesday." She pushed a button on her phone, took out the earpiece and tossed it to her desk, blew air out between her lips to release the emotional life that had come with the phone call and turned to Daniel. "Sit down. Did Tess offer you something to drink?"

"Yes."

Lindsay threw Tess a New Yorker's nod, up first, then back to neutral and Tess left, closing the door. "I'm sorry that took so long."

"Okay."

"But I wish you wouldn't do that to Tess."

"What did I do to Tess?"

"You know. The whole, 'I'm her brother' power play."

"I didn't do that."

"You know what I mean. 'I'm very important. I have places to go, things to do! I can't wait ten minutes for my sister to get off the phone!'"

"Forty-five."

"What?"

"We were supposed to meet at one-thirty."

"Shit."

"Yeah."

"Well, I said I was sorry. I don't know what you expect me to do about it."

"I said it was okay."

"It was the network."

"Yes."

"TNT."

"Yes. I know what network you're on."

"I'm just saying."

"Also, it's on the poster in your waiting area. And, you know, the building."

"Okay."

"And the visitor's badge they made me wear at the front desk."

"Are you just going to keep listing places that the network logo shows up?"

"I'm just saying."

"'Cause really you can just type up that list and e-mail it to me later."

"All right."

"I'll read it carefully. With rapt attention."

Daniel sat down. He hoped that his sister did not hear the slight gurgle that came from his stomach. "You saw Mom and Dad."

Lindsay chuckled. "Yeah. They really don't change much."

"Mom called to tell me I should get in touch with you. Apparently, you're a bigwig and might be able to help me get a job."

"She said that?"

"Yeah."

"Jesus. I'm sorry she does that to you."

"Yeah."

They sat for a minute with that hanging in the room. "I don't remember what we're supposed to be meeting about."

"Seriously?"

"Sorry. No. I mean, I remember we put it on the calendar and I was looking forward to seeing you but—"

"I asked you to look at my spec?"

"Right! Right! I did. I read the whole thing."

"The . . . whole thing?"

"Yeah! There's some nice work there. You really got the feel of the show, the pacing. The character dialogue is dead on. Nice job."

Daniel didn't know what to do with that. He felt he should thank her for the compliment, but he hadn't sent her the spec script in hope of flattery.

Lindsay didn't seem to notice the pause. "Of course, a lot of it built from the season one story line so the show's really moved on from there. Like, I remember at one point you have Mac, the janitor walk by in the background of a scene in the auditorium and he got killed off three episodes ago now."

"Yeah. When I originally sent it to you, you were only halfway through the first season."

"Right. Wow. I'm sorry it took me so long to get to it."

"Okay."

"But I'm telling you. It's really good."

"I could do an update. The stand-alone storyline holds together even if we have to change some of the timeline to fit into the current arc."

"I don't think you need to. If you're going to use it as a sample for agents or whatever, you should just put in a first page that says where it falls in the first season, so they don't think you're not aware of the contiguous nature of the show. I think you should send it out."

"Send it out."

"Yeah! Why not?"

"To agents."

"What am I missing?"

"When I asked you if I could send in a spec for the show you said I would have to send it through an agent."

"Yeah."

"For legal reasons, you said."

"Sure. They're very strict about that."

"So. . . I have an agent. I had my agent send it to you."

"That's not—didn't it come from—?" She fumbled through a pile of scripts and pulled his out from the stack to look at the cover page. "It came from Witzend Talent Agency, Daniel."

"Yes. Louis Gretch is my agent there."

"They do comedy booking and stuff for you, right?"

"Yes. They also send out my writing when I need them

to."

"Well, sure. But Daniel, they're not a proper literary agent. You know that, right?"

"Yeah. But . . . they can send stuff out for me. So it's not coming in unsolicited or whatever."

"Right. Yeah. That's why I was able to read it. But nobody's gonna take you seriously as a television writer if you have some little comedy agent sending out your stuff. You need to have an actual literary agent if you want to get staff jobs or what have you."

"You remember when you were living in that little studio apartment and you used to come over to my place to smoke my grass and watch TV in the air conditioning."

Lindsay chuckled easily. "I do. We've come a long way, haven't we, kiddo?"

"I used to let you stay there when I was on the road."

"Yeah. Jeeze. I was so scared all the time back then. I had no idea what I was doing."

"Right. Yeah."

Lindsay soaked in the soft nostalgia of familial history.

"I got back from Austin and you had read every spec script I had ever written. You said it was like a crash course in television writing and three weeks later you handed me the first draft of your first spec script."

"El Paso," Lindsay said.

"No. It was a *Full House.*"

"No. You weren't in Austin. You were in El Paso. You brought me a tee shirt from the Comic Strip."

"Right."

"That was the script that got me in at William Morris."

"Well . . ."

"What?"

"I talked you through a pretty solid rewrite of the thing."

"What?"

"I mean—you'd written it with the act breaks structured like nineteen seventies primetime, it ran eight pages long and there were two whole scenes that had nothing to do with the storyline."

"Right. Wow. That script really stuck with you."

"Also, I gave you a lot of joke punch up."

"Wait. Wait. Are you trying to take credit for the script that got me my first agent?"

"That's not—no. That's not what I'm saying."

"Because it's not like I didn't have to write three more spec scripts after that before I got my first job."

"I'm not saying that, Linds. That's not what I'm—never mind. Let's just go. Okay? Forget it."

"There was a while there that I thought I was never going to get anywhere with the writing."

"Yeah. Eight, nine whole months before that first job."

"Right? And then it would be another three before I got my first episode on. Jesus. I was so angry with you."

"What?"

"You were off doing stand-up, making a living, travelling around and I was stuck in that little apartment feeling like a talentless fraud. I don't know how you do it, kiddo."

"Wait. What?"

"Look, I've been trying not to say it, but . . . I don't know why you'd want to get into this business at all. I mean, your scripts are great. I've always said that. You match the voice of every show I've ever seen you do a spec for. But this place is a fucking formula factory, you know?

I'm getting notes from the network that are all about how they want me to make my show more like some other show that they just heard got good ratings, while over there some exec is telling their show runner that they have to make their show more like mine. It's like some incestuous, ridiculous imitation festival. If I could do what you do, I'd be doing El Paso and Austin and Tempe and Seattle and wherever and never set foot in this stupid town again. I mean, the money's great but there's just nothing real in it. You know?"

"Right. Sorry."

"What does that mean?"

"I forgot. You saw Mom and Dad recently."

Lindsay made a snorting noise that made Daniel want to comfort her.

"Did she give you a complex mathematical proof that she's not an alcoholic?"

"Several. At one point, she told me that she knows she's not an alcoholic 'cause she only has two drinks a night. One more than that and she passes out in the bathroom."

"Christ."

"It wasn't 'til the flight home that I thought I should have said, 'So, you're not an alcoholic 'cause every night you only drink yourself two thirds of the way to a blackout?"

Daniel shook his head. "Did she only have two?"

"Three. But the first one didn't count or something."

They sat with that for a moment and then Daniel said, "Look. I'm sorry if I got weird there for a minute."

"What? When?"

"Never mind. Let's just go."

"You said that before. Where are we going?"

Daniel tilted his head to the side, confused and asked, "Lunch?"

"Oh! Were we supposed to be having lunch?"

"Yeah. We're supposed to have lunch and talk about the script I wrote for your show."

"Oh." She winced.

"At one-thirty."

"I just had a whole salad while I was on with the network."

"Oh. Yeah. I was thinking lunch."

"You wouldn't believe how busy it gets."

"Yeah."

"Oh, well. Next time we'll do lunch. I promise. And I'll buy." She pushed a button on her phone and held the Bluetooth near her face without putting it in her ear. She said, "Tess, could you bring me the list of calls I need to return?"

Daniel stood. He moved toward the door and as he reached for it, Tess opened it, forcing him to step back awkwardly. She dropped a sheet of paper on Lindsay's desk and moved to step through the door behind Daniel and close it.

Daniel got halfway across the waiting area before going back to Tess's cubicle. He held out his parking ticket for her to stamp

He said, "I almost forgot. I need validation."

LATE

Daniel slid into the rental car. He placed the contract he had just been handed on the passenger's seat so he would have it ready when he drove by the little check-the-rental-contract booth at the exit.

He had shoved his travel bag into the back seat but not before pulling a USB cable from the outer pocket. He searched around the car's console. When he found the USB port, he plugged the cable in and then pushed the mini-end into his phone. He tried placing the phone on the dashboard, but he could tell that would slide around when he turned. He inverted it into the cup holder but realized immediately that it would be impossible to see the map as he navigated. He turned around to face the back of the car, knelt on the driver's seat and reached into the bag to find a rolled-up pair of socks. He used them to hold the cable to the bottom of the cup holder and hold his phone upright where he would be able to glance at it if he needed to.

He started the car with the discomfort he always felt when he rented one of the new models that had a button and a radio frequency fob instead of a proper keyhole ignition. He adjusted his seat's position. He adjusted his rear-view mirror. He adjusted the temperature settings. He set the radio pre-set buttons to the two NPR stations he knew came in here.

He said, "Ok, Google," and waited for the "bloop" from his phone that meant Google was ready to listen to his command. "Navigate to Mom and Dad's place."

"Okay! Navigating to Mom and Dad." After a moment she added, "Exit the parking garage and turn left."

"Thank you, Sacajawea." Daniel said this every time he remembered to do it when the navigator spoke. He almost never had an opportunity to do it in front of anyone else, so it was really just a joke he did for himself. He very much wanted to get the navigator to respond to "Ok, Sacajawea," instead of "Ok, Google," but hacking software wasn't anything he knew how to do and he certainly wasn't going to spend a bunch of time learning how to do it or hiring someone to do it for him.

When he found himself considering googling for a YouTube how-to video right that minute on his phone, he knew that he was stalling. He let out a long breath and pulled out of the parking space.

His plane had landed more than an hour late, which wasn't all that bad considering the fact that his plane had taken off more than an hour and a half late. He had texted his parents from the tarmac in L.A. to tell them that it looked like he'd be late arriving, and they had told him not to call when he landed as they might be asleep. His mother had called as soon as he texted her. "Just come straight from the airport. If we're going to sleep, we'll just leave the door unlocked and you can let yourself in and lock it behind you. If it's locked, it means we're still up and you can just ring the bell and we'll let you in. Easy-peasy."

"You know you could have just texted back at me."

"I know. But that seems like such a lot of trouble when I can just ring you up and say what I have to say."

"Okay."

"I'm so glad you're coming to stay here instead of going to some awful hotel."

"I'm looking forward to it. It'll be good."

"Right? We almost never get to see you."

"Okay. I'll be there in, you know, a bunch of hours."

"Fly safely!"

"Oh, I don't think they'll be putting me in charge."

"You know your father always says that?"

Daniel told her that he did know that. Then they had hung up.

Now he was stalling. He wanted them to be asleep. He wanted to let himself in, go to the guest room and not have to have a conversation, not have to hug and hear about how much taller he seemed than she remembered, not have to explain why he was in Boston. He wished, for the two-hundredth time that he had gotten a hotel room. It was a business trip. He could write off the expense and he was making enough on this deal to cover a little bit of comfort for himself.

He had decided to save money and guilt. He told his parents he would stay in the guest room in their apartment on Memorial Drive. Condo. They liked to call it a condo. Every time he said apartment, one or the other of them would say, "It's a condo." He tried to remember to use the language they liked because he didn't like the tone with which they corrected him. They lived in a condo. On the eighteenth floor of a tall apartment building.

He had thanked Sacajawea several times for her

instructions when he failed to make a slight left and she announced that she was recalculating. He thanked her and drove in silence waiting for her to direct him. When she did, he thanked her.

He followed her direction until he made a wrong turn again and then he again allowed her to re-map his route for him.

He parked in one of the spots designated for visitors and went to the front door of the building. He tapped on the glass so that the guy behind the security desk noticed him and buzzed him in. He was never sure whether the guy was a guard or a doorman or what. He waved to him as he pulled his rolling luggage behind him through the front entrance. The guy said, "You're Daniel Grunman?"

"Yeah."

The guy chuckled.

"Wow. You're an easy laugh, man."

"Your mother told me you were coming. I sort of thought you were—you know—a kid. Twenties. You know?"

"Based on her age?"

The guy choked a little bit. "Right. Didn't really think about that. Just, you know, the way she talks about you."

"I don't know how she talks about me. I know how she talks *to* me and that's really as much as I can take. How does she talk about me?"

"Oh, you know. She calls you her youngest. Says you're a talented kid but you smoke too much pot. That sort of thing."

"She knows I quit smoking pot."

"Okay."

"More than ten years ago."

"Okay. Also, you're not really a kid so much."

"Right?"

"Wow. When you say that, though, you sound just like her."

"Okay." He headed to the elevator and pushed the button for his parents' floor. He leaned against the wall of the elevator and rested his hand on the handle of his luggage. He watched the numbers change as he passed the floors.

He hoped the door would be unlocked when he got there.

He stepped off the elevator, realized he had left his luggage behind, spun around in time to stop the door from closing and have a brief imagining of the sensor not working so that the machinery would crush his hand and then, when that did not occur, retrieved the bag. He listened to the soft hush of his suitcase wheels on the carpet as he walked the hallway.

He took a moment to hope again that the door would be unlocked as he reached for the knob. It did not turn. He sighed. He paused. He considered waiting until he heard the door unlock and then waiting another fifteen minutes and then letting himself in and going straight to the guest room. He rang the bell.

From inside he heard his mother shout, "Hang on! Hang on, Honey! I'm coming. Don't go anywhere."

Although he could only make out enough of his father's voice to catch the inflection, he knew what the man was saying. "Where's he gonna go? You think he's going to book a flight back home if you don't answer the door fast enough?"

He heard footsteps on the wooden floorboards of the

entryway. He heard the clicking of the deadbolt. The doorknob jiggled. Then the deadbolt clicked again. Then the doorknob jiggled. Mom shouted, "Hang on! Just give me a second. Don't go anywhere!"

Daniel shouted, "Where am I going to go?"

The deadbolt clicked again. Paul said something in the muffled distance that Daniel knew to be an explanation of the latch lock controlled by the button at the middle of the doorknob.

Mom shouted. "Very funny. This always takes me a second. Just stay put."

"You think I'm going to book a flight back home if you don't answer the door fast enough?"

Mom shouted, "Your father just said the same thing."

"You don't have to yell. I'm right on the other side of the door."

Mom shouted, "What?"

Dad, in the distance, repeated what Daniel had just told her. Then the door opened and the visit began.

Daniel crossed the threshold into air long-saturated with the smell of fried food and Merit cigarettes. He opened his arms wide and hugged a little bit less than he allowed himself to be hugged.

Ellen said, "Oh, it is so good to see you."

"You can't see me. The side of your whole face is pressed up against my chest."

"Right you are. Right you are." She did not stop hugging him. She held on for significantly longer than Daniel felt comfortable being held on to. He used one hand to fumble behind himself until he found the edge of the door and swung it closed with a thump and a click. He hoped that sound would be enough to signal the end of the embrace. Instead, Ellen pulled back just enough to look at his face. She rearranged his hair in a way that felt to him entirely too intimate for the mother-son relationship. "When did you get this tall?"

"About twenty-three years ago."

"I don't remember you being this tall."

"I know. You never do."

"I used to carry you around."

"You want to carry me around again? 'Cause if you want to try, I'm pretty tired."

"Don't be funny."

Paul joined them in the tiny alcove of a foyer. "That's a terrible thing to say to a comic."

"Comedian."

"Comedian."

Ellen said, "What's the difference?"

Daniel said, "Cufflinks. If I have to stay in the foyer, I'm going to need a blanket or at least a big towel."

"Don't be silly. Why would we make you stay in the foyer?"

"Ellen."

"I have no idea, but you don't seem to be letting me come into the apartment."

"Oh!" Ellen backed up so she was no longer keeping her son in place and took him by the hand to lead him into the wide expanse of the living room/dining room space. Daniel wondered why he allowed it, but he allowed it.

"You got a bunch of different furniture since I was here last."

Ellen beamed. "No. Reupholstered the couch and then had the reading chairs done to match. And we rearranged it a bit for better light and flow."

"Flow?"

"I heard a thing about Feng Shui on NPR."

Daniel nodded.

Paul said, "I call the design style 'urban sprawl.'"

"Nice."

Ellen said, "I don't think that's really a design style."

"Ellen."

"You should have a conversation with the people who design traffic in Boston," Daniel suggested. "The flow is terrible."

Paul said, "It's a pain in the ass, isn't it? They do it that way 'cause they figure if you don't live here, you don't deserve to get where you're going."

"Oh, I don't think it's conscious, Paul. Do you? I just think Boston came together as a metropolis in the days before urban planning was a thing."

"You're probably right, Dear. You're probably right." He exchanged a look with Daniel, who tried not to laugh.

"Well, whatever the reason, it's maddening. The GPS navigator in my phone was reduced to stammering apologies."

"That's silly. It's not really programmed to do that, is it? Does ours do that, Paul? I almost never use it."

"Are you kidding? By the third time I missed the soft right to get me back to Memorial Drive it wasn't even giving directions. It was just screaming obscenities at me."

Ellen slapped at his arm playfully to suggest that she was certain now that he was kidding.

They moved together toward the small breakfast table, the only table Paul and Ellen ever used when they were not entertaining guests. Despite setting him up in the guest room, they did not think of Daniel as a guest. Daniel felt entirely okay about that. Sitting at the breakfast table seemed natural to him, wholly familiar, familial.

Paul said, "You want a drink?"

"No. Thanks. I'm okay."

"Well I'm going to have a last one. Ellen?"

"What the hell. Sure." Then she spoke earnestly to Daniel, "I don't usually have more than two."

"So you've said."

"But we started Scrabble early today so it should be fine."

Daniel heard the sentence for the gibberish it was. He also knew exactly what she meant. She meant that their daily Scrabble games had started early which meant that her first drink had come earlier than usual. She felt, therefore, that she'd had more time since her first drink than usual and could allow herself another. He also knew that the number of drinks was not affected by the size of the drinks, that some drinks could be discounted based on brand or temperature, and that the more drinks she had the more proofs she would be likely to offer that she was not an alcoholic.

While Paul poured scotch over ice, Daniel moved past him to get a glass of water.

Paul said, "I thought you didn't want anything."

"It's just water."

"Ice?"

"Sure." He held out the glass. His father dropped in a couple of cubes.

Ellen said, "I'm not even usually up this late. So, sure. Why not? One more."

Daniel said, "You know you're allowed to stay up late and not have a drink."

Paul said, "Daniel."

Ellen said, "Don't be silly. I don't mind."

Paul glared at his son.

They sat together at the table, ice clinking in glasses.

Paul peered into his drink as though he was reading his future in the array of his ice cubes. Ellen gazed at her son as though she saw the child he had once been and hoped to see through time to what he would look like as a grown up.

"I didn't think you two would still be up when I got here."

"Yeah. We waited up."

"I'm touched."

"I can't believe how tall you've gotten."

"Ellen."

Daniel said, "If you want to do this scene again we should reset to the entryway."

Ellen said, "What?"

"Doesn't matter. Thanks for letting me stay here while I'm in town."

Paul said, "You always have a home here if you need it. You know. Briefly."

Daniel chuckled.

"Paul." She turned to Daniel and said, "You are welcome to stay here any time you want for as long as you want."

"Thanks, Mom. But really, the two days is about all any of us can handle."

Ellen sipped her scotch. "Oooh. This is good. This isn't the Jameson."

"It's the scotch."

"It's the good scotch."

"Yes."

Daniel sipped his water. He felt an ice cube bounce against his upper lip.

Ellen said, "So, you're in town for work."

"Yes. Yes I am."

"But you're not doing one of your little comedy gigs."

"No. And I generally just refer to them as gigs."

Paul said, "Are you being deliberately oblique? Is there some sort of secret about what you're doing?"

Daniel sighed. "No. It's not a big secret. I'm ghost writing, so it's a little secret. I have to spend a couple of days interviewing the guy so I can write his autobiography."

Ellen said, "Ooooh. Who is it?"

"That's the part that has to be a secret."

"Why is that?" Ellen asked.

"Because that's how ghost-writing works. It's a politician who needs to have a book out and knows how to sell a book but doesn't know how to write a book."

"So, you have to write it for him?"

"No, Mom. I *get* to write it for him and I get to be paid pretty damn well for it."

Ellen's eyes widened. She reached across the table and put a hand on his. "Oh, that sounds terrific! And if that gets published you get into the Writers' Guild, right?"

"What?"

"Like your sister did? The Writers' Guild. That's what it was called, isn't it, Paul?"

"Yeah. That was for that situation comedy thing that she wrote."

"God that thing was awful."

Daniel said, "No. No, ghost writing a politician's

autobiography will not get me into the Writers' Guild."

Paul said, "That's a shame. Your sister's been making a good living, I think, since she got into that Guild."

"Yes. Yes, she has."

Ellen said, "I don't understand why this doesn't get you in. A book is a lot harder than a silly little sitcom."

"Well, first of all, Guild qualification isn't based on level of difficulty. Secondly, I'm not getting credit on the book, so even if it *could* qualify me—"

"I don't like that. You should really ask to get credit for your work."

"Ellen, that's not how ghost-writing works."

"Well I don't think that's right."

"And thirdly the WGA is for screenwriters. You don't get in for writing a book."

Ellen said, "Really? I figured if you had a book published, you'd be allowed in."

Daniel paused. He sipped his water. He said, "No. No." He looked to his father, but Paul stared into his drink. Daniel said slowly, "And . . . I've already had two books published."

Ellen laughed lightly. "Oh, honey. Of course you have. I don't think of those as real books."

Daniel blinked. He knew that she thought what she had said would serve as a course correction. He knew that she believed, somehow, that what she had just said was an apology. Daniel said, "Seriously?"

"What?"

Paul said, "Come on, Daniel. Don't do that."

Daniel looked to him in disbelief.

Paul, answering the unvoiced outrage, said, "They both came out through that one little publisher. It might as well have been a vanity press."

"It's a boutique publisher. It isn't a vanity press."

"Okay."

"And you know, in modern America, self-publishing is considered entrepreneurial."

"Okay. Look, you can tell yourself whatever you want about your books, but you don't get to be mad at your mother if she doesn't think of them as some huge accomplishment."

"Huge accomplishment? She forgot they existed."

"And she apologized for that."

"When?"

Ellen said, "Just now. You heard me."

Daniel shook his head slowly. He sipped his water. He considered going out into the hall and waiting until his parents unlocked the door for him and went to bed.

Paul turned his glass on its coaster. "I don't understand what just happened."

Daniel said, "Never mind. It doesn't matter."

"All your mother was saying—"

"I know what she was saying."

Paul started again, allowing his voice to turn stern and instructional. "All your mother was saying was that she wants you to get the credit you deserve."

"Okay."

"Don't dismiss it like that, Daniel. You know, we all hear what we want to hear. I read a piece in *Psychology Today* about the way we talk past one another and I think sometimes we hear what we expect to hear and not what's actually said, not what's intended."

"Okay."

"Your mother feels—and I feel it too—that there's

something inherently wrong about you not getting credit when you're finally actually working on what might be a proper book that I assume will be coming out from a real publishing company."

"Okay." Then, more quietly, he said, "Jesus."

"I don't understand why this seems to be upsetting you so much. You understand that we're on your side, right?"

"Yes. I do. I get that." But he shook his head from side to side, trying hard to dismiss the stinging comments.

"So, good. We're all on the same page."

"Okay."

They sat in silence for a moment.

Paul moved his coaster and his drink to the side.

Ellen said, "Really?"

"Sure. We're up."

Ellen brought out the scrabble board and unfolded it onto the center of the table. She picked a tile from the bag and held it up for Paul to see. She offered the bag to Daniel. He said, "No, thanks."

Paul said, "I don't understand." They all laughed lightly at Paul's feigned bafflement. Paul pulled a tile from the bag and showed it to his wife. She handed him the bag. He drew his first seven letters. "So far, so good."

Daniel drank water. He finished the glass and went to refill it.

Ellen said, "You're thirsty."

"Yeah. Flying always leaves me dehydrated."

"Okay."

"What does that mean?"

"I worry."

"Ellen. Don't do that."

"What am I doing?"

"You're fishing. If you want to ask, just ask."

Daniel said, "Jesus."

Paul said, "Have you noticed that we say, 'Jesus' a lot for a family of atheist Jews?"

"I haven't. But I should write a bit about it. There's something there."

Ellen said, "Just don't go all vulgar and shock value with it."

"Okay."

Paul played a word and Ellen tallied his score. She arranged the tiles on her rack. As if it were just a stray thought that had crossed her mind she asked, "So, are you still not smoking pot?"

"I quit smoking pot eleven and a half years ago."

"Well good. Good for you."

"Everyone gets dehydrated when they fly."

"Okay. It's fine. I believe you." She sipped her scotch.

"Look. It's late. I should probably get to bed."

Paul said, "Is that 'cause we started playing? We can put the game away."

"Hah!" Ellen put all seven of her letters on the board to form a word. She marked her score on the score sheet. "The hell we can."

"Well certainly not *now*." Paul studied his letters intently.

"No. It's not because you started playing. I'm just— travel is exhausting."

Paul said, "Isn't it? Also, it messes with my digestion. Do you get travel stomach?"

"Yeah. And the constant sense of disorientation is troubling. You know you guys keep your ocean in the wrong direction?"

Ellen said, "That's 'cause we're on the whole other coast."

"Yes."

"Don't narrate the jokes, Honey."

"I thought I was bantering."

Paul snorted and played a word.

"Also when I travel, I find myself constantly checking my pockets like Columbo arriving at a crime scene."

"I loved that show." Ellen played a word and added the score.

"You loved the character. You hated the show."

"Well, yes. I hated the format. It was so stupid. We know who committed the crime, he knows who committed the crime, and then it's just two hours of head games."

Daniel said, "It's Dostoevsky."

Ellen said, "What?"

Paul said, "Huh."

"Every episode of the original series was a reworking of *Crime and Punishment*."

"Wow. That's right. I think that's right." Paul moved the letters around on his tray, studying the combinations.

"Then the show went off the air and they started doing the occasional M.O.W.s and—"

Paul said, "What are M.O.W.s?"

"Oooh!" Ellen raised her hand like a schoolgirl showing off that she had done the homework. "I know this. I read this somewhere. It means 'without sound,' but I don't remember why."

"No. That's M.O.S., Mom. M.O.W.s are Movies of the Week. And at that point they started hiring in regular, network approved writers from their own crime dramas and none of them understood how to make the format work so they got them all wrong. Columbo was just another detective, figuring it out as he went along instead of knowing right from the beginning and using the investigation to trap the killer in his own arrogance."

Paul shook his head in amazement. "Dostoevsky. I can't believe I never put that together before."

He took his glass to refill it. Ellen held her glass up for him and when he took it, she gestured with her finger and thumb close together to suggest that he should pour a very little bit for her. She explained to her son, "I don't really need any more, but that's just such good scotch."

"Okay."

Paul returned to the table and gave Ellen her refreshed drink. She sipped.

Paul said, "You really seem to have a strong understanding of this TV writing stuff."

"Yeah."

"Why don't you pick up some of that work?"

"I would love to. I've been doing spec scripts for years."

Ellen said, "Is that a show?"

"Is what a show?"

"Spec. Is that the show where the two boys in San Diego pretend to be clairvoyant?"

"That's *Psych*. And it's set in Santa Barbara. And only one of them pretends to be psychic. Spec scripts are scripts written for extant shows as work samples. They're still called 'spec scripts' 'cause people used to write them on speculation hoping to sell them to the series. It doesn't really work that way anymore, though,"

"I enjoy that show. I think they're funny, those boys."

"Yes. Yes, they are."

Paul said, "Have you talked to Lindsay?"

"All the time."

"No. I mean, about this."

"I should talk to Lindsay about how Mom enjoys *Psych* without seeming to understand any of its most basic elements?"

Ellen said, "Don't be funny."

"You really have to stop saying that, Ellen."

"What did I say?"

"You remember when my third-grade teacher said, 'Don't get smart with me, young man,' and I said, 'There's very little chance of that happening,' and then I had to go to the principal's office?"

Ellen said, "I do. I came down and stuck up for you."

"Yes."

"I couldn't believe that. What a terrible thing for any teacher to say to a student."

"Right. That's what Dad means when he says that you should stop telling me not to be funny."

Ellen played a word. She added her score. She sipped her drink. She shrugged in a way that suggested she was unimpressed by the analogy. "Do you know that I was in therapy for five months last night?"

"What?"

"I was in therapy."

"For five months last night?"

"Last year."

"Okay."

"I said last year."

"Okay."

"You heard me, Paul."

"I'm sorry. I wasn't really—" He played a word. Ellen

added his score.

"Why are you telling me about therapy?"

"Hang on." Ellen played a word quickly. As she picked new letters, her hand searching in the bag for tiles, she said, "I was very worried that I had been a terrible, terrible mother. To both of you. Not just your sister. Both of you."

"Okay."

"He introduced me to the idea of the 'good enough mother'. I wasn't perfect, but you turned out okay. Right? So, I was a good enough mother. I was finally able to stop with the self-recrimination."

"Good. Good for you."

"So, I think it would be very helpful to me if you would stop with the accusations."

"Honey, nobody was accusing you of anything."

"Well, I'm pretty sure Daniel was just trying to compare me to that awful teacher he had back in third grade."

"That's not exactly what I said."

"Well, maybe you should think about how people around you are going to hear what you say before you say it. That's all I'm saying." Then, with an off-timed wave of dismissal she repeated, "That's all I'm saying."

Daniel sipped his water. He pulled an ice cube into his mouth and shattered it between his teeth. He let the shards melt against the warmth of his tongue. "You promise?"

"Daniel."

Ellen said, "What? What did I miss?"

Paul played a word and Ellen scored it.

Daniel looked into his glass of water, then recognized it as his father's mannerism and stopped. He set his glass on a coaster and turned it with his fingertips. He recognized that as well and stopped. He put his hands on his lap and felt awkward.

Paul said, "You haven't gone to bed."

"Yeah."

Ellen said, "Are you sure you don't want a drink?"

"Yeah."

Paul said, "Do you mind if we put on NPR?"

"Could you not?"

"Okay."

The game continued in silence for a few turns. Then Ellen, tentatively said, "So, when do you start work?"

"Tomorrow morning I'll be up early to drive out to the Cape for the day."

"Cape Cod? That's a drive. Make sure you leave enough time."

Paul said, "You'll be going against the traffic. It shouldn't be too bad."

Ellen said, "You should still make sure you leave enough time. You don't want to be late for your first day of school."

"Work."

"What?"

"I'm driving to Cape Cod for work. Not for school."

"Okay."

"I'll get directions from my phone. It estimates drive times pretty accurately."

"I love the way people just carry their phones around with them everywhere now."

Paul said, "I have a smart phone, but I don't think I'm smart enough to use it right."

"You know, when you were a boy, Daniel, we didn't

even have an answering machine. If someone called and you weren't home, it just rang until they gave up. If it was important, they'd just call back later."

"Good story," Daniel said.

"Daniel."

Daniel sighed. "You don't have a cell phone, Mom?"

"I have one. It's not the fancy kind like you and your father have, but I don't really need all of that fancy stuff."

"Yeah. But it's good that you have one. Just in case."

Ellen went on. "Of course, I don't carry it around with me everywhere I go like the kids do now. I mostly just leave it in the little charging stand by the door."

"Wait. You don't take it with you when you go out?"

"No. I really only have it for emergencies."

Daniel blinked slowly, writing jokes in his head. Mean jokes. Cutting jokes.

Paul said, "Daniel."

"What did he say?"

"He didn't." He glared at Daniel.

Daniel said, "Jesus."

"What did I miss?"

Daniel sipped his water. Paul sipped his scotch. Ellen lifted her glass to her lips, realized it was empty and set it back down with a slightly furrowed brow.

Paul said, "More?"

"I don't really need any." Then she sighed.

Paul took her glass and poured more scotch. He returned it to her.

Ellen said, "You really are a terrible influence."

"Yes."

Daniel said, "Jesus, you guys. Do you even see yourselves? Do you—is there any self-awareness here at all? You sit here in a fucking haze playing Scrabble exactly the way you have every day since I was five, hardly talking to one another and pretending that stasis is the same thing as happiness."

Paul played a word and shifted his focus from the board to his son. Ellen scored the word, slid the bag of letters toward Paul, and studied the letters on her rack.

Paul said, "Where is this coming from?"

Ellen said, "You know what? You really have no right to sit there in judgment of us."

Daniel stood up. He started talking. He repressed the impulse, turned to go to bed. Changed his mind and turned back. "In judgment of you? I can't judge you? I've been sitting here feeling like I'm barely on your radar, absorbing body-blows of judgmentalism. My books aren't real. My ghost-writing gig isn't good enough 'cause I'm not getting credit for it. I shouldn't be funny, which is—you know—my career. Also, I shouldn't be vulgar even though that's really not what I do anyway. And then suddenly it's like I'm sitting through some boozy production of a lost Pinter play."

"Oh. Look, Ellen. It's Daniel Grunman playing Daniel Grunman—the role of a lifetime."

"Paul, that's not nice. I think Daniel is really upset."

"You think?"

"Well you certainly sound upset."

"Ellen."

"Yeah. Okay. Never mind."

Ellen said, "Is there something you want to talk about, Honey? Because I don't think what you're upset about is really what you're saying it's about."

"What?"

"Do you know why I think you're such a little grumpy pants?"

"'Such a little grumpy pants?'"

"Don't infantilize, Ellen."

"I think you're upset because we mentioned how well your sister is doing and you're a little bit jealous, that's what I think. She's got her television show on the Dynamite Channel and she's getting all this money and whatever else and you're still just traveling around doing your little comedy skits and picking up jobs writing other people's books for them."

"Okay."

"She could be right, Daniel."

"Okay."

"You know, your mother's not entirely out of left field here. And it's not your sister's fault you wasted all that time hanging around in Hollywood getting stoned when you could have been developing a career."

Daniel thought about how much of his pot Lindsay had smoked over her first years in Los Angeles. "Okay."

Ellen played a word and added the score.

Paul shifted his letters around in his rack.

Daniel felt his eyebrows moving and realized he was having a whole conversation in his head.

Ellen sipped her drink.

Paul played a word and while Ellen added his score, he crossed the room to the stereo system. He turned on National Public Radio and a woman's voice began to drone on about the technicalities of parliamentary procedure being used to prevent a bill from reaching the floor for a vote.

Paul sat back down and picked new letters from the

bag. "Only three left."

Ellen said, "Okay."

"Yeah. I'm gonna go to bed." Daniel stood up.

Paul pushed his seat back and stood up. "Okay. We should be up in the morning but if we oversleep, just let yourself out and let the latch lock behind you. Ring us when you have a sense of when you're getting back tomorrow. Yeah?"

"Okay."

Paul pulled him into a drunken hug. "It really is good to see you."

"Yeah."

Paul sat back down. Ellen stood up and hugged him. "I'm sorry you got so upset."

"Okay."

She released him, took half a step back. "I just can't believe how tall you've gotten."

"It's constantly shocking to me too."

"Okay." She stumbled backward a bit, her calves bumping against her chair. She put a hand on the table to stabilize. "I must be tired. That scotch is really hitting me."

Paul said, "I'm sure you are. It's pretty late."

"Okay. Good night guys."

Daniel grabbed his rolling bag and headed toward the guest room. Paul barked, "Lift that up, would you? I don't like the wheel tracks on the hardwood."

"Yeah. Okay." He collapsed the extendable handle and lifted the bag.

Alone in the guest room, he sat for a moment, the only sound the radio, murmuring distantly, soothing and soft.

He thought about the visits over the years, the subtle jabs, the unconscious attacks. He remembered the slights he had endured in silence when he was broke and needed money too much to risk rocking the boat. He remembered the drunken lectures about how he should stop smoking pot. He remembered seething in silence through the carefully worded conversations about how many artists find a stable life in academia.

He muttered to himself, "That was relatively painless," and felt a wry smile tug at the corner of his mouth. It certainly hadn't been as bad as it could have been, as bad as it had been sometimes in the past. Still, he felt an angry clenching in his solar plexus. A hollow sadness threatened to pull him into a small, fragile ball.

A knock at his door startled him and he flinched. "Yeah?"

The door opened. His mother stood in the doorway. It was an image that harkened back to his childhood, her figure framed and backlit, the last goodnight. "I folded some towels in the bathroom for you. You'll see them."

"Thanks."

"If you get cold—"

"I won't."

"—there's an extra blanket on the top shelf in the closet."

"I know where it is."

"Okay." Ellen stood there, gazing at her adult son, trying to see back through time to the child he had once been. "I feel like I should offer to read you a story."

"Yeah. Yeah I get that."

"I love you. You know that, right?"

He wanted to say that he loved her too, but it felt too much as though she was asking for him to, too much as though it would be a concession. All he could manage was,

"Yeah. I know. Me too."

She nodded. He wondered what she was looking for as she tilted her head a bit to the side and studied him. She leaned against the door frame and sighed. She said, "It's so late. How did it get so late?"

GIFT

Darling Lindsay,

Happy anniversary. It's hard to believe it's already been fifteen years since you and that lovely woman got together. I hope you know how much we adore her, and I hope she knows as well.

It took me a while to find just the right gift for you. I went all the way out to the mall and then schlepped around from store to store looking at things and just thinking about you and what I could remember from that last visit to your house, trying to think of what you might need to make the place feel homier, more like a nice place to raise a family.

(Your father wants me to cut that last sentence because he thinks it sounds like I'm hinting about grand-children, but I swear to you, I'm not. I got that message loud and clear, although, to be completely truthful, I don't know why you won't even think about it. I mean, there are all sorts of ways now for one of you to get pregnant and if that doesn't appeal to you, adoption is always a perfectly good option. I remember when you told me that you two aren't going to have kids because you do not like children; I thought, "Oh! She gets that from me!" It's not as though everyone who has ever had children has felt entirely prepared. I certainly didn't, and I must have done something right; just look how great you and your brother turned out!)

Naturally, the first thing I thought of was to get you a new bed for the guest room to replace that horrible lumpy convertible couch you had me and your father sleep on when we came out there, but I was afraid that would seem too much like something I was doing to make myself more comfortable in case I ever visit again and for whatever reason don't opt for a comfortable hotel room to stay in. Besides, I had no idea how expensive a bed can be until I started looking for one and that just seemed an outrageous expense for something to send you that might only be used on special occasions. I don't know; do you ever even have visitors when your father and I aren't out there on one of our rare cross-country excursions? It's funny to think of you having a whole life out in California all the time when we're not even there, going out to dinner and taking out the trash and doing all those things that grown up people do.

I could have shopped for a present "on line" as they say. That's where you buy things over the computer. It really is amazing. You just type in all your credit card information, all those little numbers, clickety clickety click and the thing you ordered just comes right to you in the mail, just like if you'd ordered it from a real catalog. I like to look at things and touch them before I buy them, though, so I went down to the mall and picked out this lovely table-setting for eight. God knows when you'd actually be serving eight whole people dinner, of course, but I noticed that some of your plates and saucers and so on didn't match when I was looking through your cabinets trying to find the wine glasses there, so I thought this was something you might be able to use. I picked it out, jotted down the product number and then went home and ordered it from my computer because everyone tells me that's so much more convenient, though, to tell you the truth, I really don't understand why.

I hope you love the place settings as much as I did when I saw them. They're all made of some sort of wonderful hardwood. I think they said it was endangered and I know you two are all environmentally conscious and everything but still, they're just lovely with the deep, rich wood grain. They can't just go in a dishwasher; you have to do them by hand. They take a special kind of detergent that won't stain the wood or take out the oils or something. I don't know. I bought a small bottle of it to be delivered along with the stuff. If you need more, it's called Tru-Grain Cleanser and when you use it you'll just want to make sure that you wipe the dishes clean thoroughly with a paper towel or a rag that you don't mind throwing out because over time it becomes toxic as it evaporates. When you run out of the bottle I sent, you can order more at a company. I don't remember what it's called, but you can look it up through the computer. We have a thing here called The Google. I don't know if you have the same thing on the West Coast but I'm sure you have something like it. It's like the old yellow pages (Oy, am I dating myself?) only it's in your computer and you can look up just about anything.

My love to you and your lovely girlfriend (Your father

says I should stop calling her that, or you'll think I can't even remember her name. Isn't that a riot?)

Mom

MEMORY'S A FUNNY THING

Daniel was not certain his father had remembered at all. Perhaps he had gotten the date wrong or written down the name of the club incorrectly. He had peered out discreetly into the crowd during the laughs and the applause breaks, but the stage lights made individuals indistinguishable. It would be typical of his father to make a big deal out of e-mailing for the information and then find a way to miss the show.

As he came off stage, he met some strangers who had enjoyed his performance, then he saw Paul awaiting his attention, small and frail in his overcoat as though the weight of the wool itself might buckle the man's aging legs. Daniel disengaged from the knot of admirers and went to his father for a hug, a moment of genuine, human connection before the familial guards came up, the tensions, the mannerisms.

They stood awkwardly for a moment, assessing one another, shuffling. "I need a cigarette. Can we . . .?" Paul trailed off with a gesture toward the door and together they stepped out of the warmth.

"You're funny."

"Thanks. I'm glad you could make it."

"You're much smarter than most of the guys who went on that stage tonight."

Daniel shrugged. He shifted his feet. He agreed, but it wasn't a thing he liked to say aloud. He preferred to mask his arrogance.

Paul sighed smoke. He blinked in a way that was almost a wince, almost a flinch. It told Daniel that he was trying not to say something or, more accurately, hoping to be coaxed.

Daniel did not know how not to oblige. "What?"

Paul feigned confusion. "What?"

"Don't do the Meisner thing with me. There was something you wanted to say."

Paul nodded. He sighed again, shifted his head from side to side for a moment as though he was weighing options. "I think you know."

Daniel thought he knew too but he'd been wrong before. He waited.

"There's a bit in there that you really have to stop doing."

Daniel had correctly surmised his father's thought. He knew which bit Paul was talking about. It was this:

The last time I visited my grandmother, Alzheimer's was just setting in. Every time she saw me, she thought it was my birthday and gave me five dollars. It was exhausting to deal with. I had to keep walking in and out of that room.

(For the record, that is not a self-loathing anti-Semitic joke about a cultural relationship with money that values it above human decency. It's a self-loathing anti-capitalist

joke about a societal relationship with money that values it above human decency.)

She had just reached that point in the progression of the disease at which every conversation turns into a surreal, nineteen-seventies television game show. She'd say, "I went into that place . . . with the buildings and the smell."

And we'd all shout, "Manhattan?"

"Yes! I was with that know-it-all lady with the flowered dress and the long boring stories."

"Your best friend Katie?"

"Yes! We saw that horrible guy!"

"We need more clues!"

"He used to be horrible in New York and then he was horrible all over the country and now he's horrible from space!"

"Howard Stern?"

"Yes!"

"Congratulations, Grandma! You're going on to the dementia pyramid!"

"WHO ARE YOU PEOPLE?"

"Things you yell at the dinner table!"

"WHERE AM I?"

"Things you shout from the bathroom!"

"Ed Asner! Benjamin Netanyahu!"

"People you mistake for your dead husband?"

"Yay, Grandma! Great clues! You're a big winner!"

I remember my mother was all freaked out, realizing that she was facing a genetic crapshoot. She said, "Daniel, you have to tell me if I start showing symptoms, so I'll know when it's time to take my own life."

I said, "Mom . . . we just had this conversation twenty

minutes ago."

Hands in his pockets, shoulders up against the cold, Daniel risked the guess. "The Alzheimer's run?"

"Yeah. It's not funny."

"It gets a lot of laughs. And a huge applause break."

"That doesn't mean it's funny," then, "It would destroy your mother if she saw it."

"She can handle more than you think."

"It's about her mother."

"Yes."

Paul pulled smoke. His pressed his lips together. "It's really offensive."

"Different people are offended by different things."

"I think you've forgotten how awful it was."

Daniel said, "No."

"It wasn't cute, Danny. It wasn't funny. It was tragic."

That was when, with absolute certainty, Daniel knew he was right and his father was wrong.

In 1974 Daniel was ten years old. He went with his parents and his sister to visit Grandma and Grandpa at their home in New Jersey for a big, tense Thanksgiving dinner, long before his Grandmother's mind began to slip. During one of the difficult pauses, while his mother bathed in a lifetime of familial subtext and his father tried to imagine how he was being judged by his in-laws, to avoid putting another bite of inedible, turkey-flavored particle board into his mouth, Daniel said, "This summer I'm going to camp! I'm gonna ride horses and learn to play guitar!"

His grandmother, still healthy in her late sixties said, "I went to a camp once."

Grandpa laughed sharply. Daniel's parents, Paul and Ellen, gasped. His sister, Lindsay, stared at her food. When things made people laugh, she went quiet as though she had to analyze every word in careful silence.

Grandma went on with barely a pause. "Spent nine months of my life in a yard full of gypsies and queers playing liar's poker." With a deliberate gesture she rolled up a sleeve to look at the numbers tattooed on her forearm. "Pair of threes." She paused, looking at an imagined opponent. "Three fives."

Grandpa laughed now in a way that was joyous and actively supportive as he saw the discomfort on the faces of Daniel's parents.

Paul said, "Stop it, Sally. That's terrible."

Ellen sighed. Paul's jaw tensed, compressing rage between his teeth. Daniel watched it all, sorting out as best he could the source of his parents' discomfort, trying to reverse engineer the back story that made his grandmother's joke so potent.

Grandpa, always ready to put horror under laughing glass, grinned at his wife. He said to Daniel's parents, or perhaps to Daniel himself, "You know, that's when I fell in love with her. Do you know how sharp you have to be to win with the same numbers every day? Besides, I always liked skinny girls."

"Come on, Man," and it sounded like some sort of warning. Paul glanced toward Daniel and Lindsay, clearly hoping his father-in-law would follow his gaze, would censor his wit for the benefit of the kids.

Grandpa would not be silenced through intimidation or outrage, though. He would not be quieted by the squeamish manners of the man who had married his daughter. "I saw her across the yard and I thought, *My god. Her tights are loose!*" He took a beat to let the shock register on the faces of Paul and Ellen before he tagged it with, "Then I realized she wasn't wearing tights."

That image made Daniel laugh a little and Grandma fell apart with giggles.

Ellen said, "Really, guys. This is wrong. Set an example. You don't make jokes about tragedy."

Grandma feigned anger but Daniel could see that she truly reveled in the moment. She smelled their offense like blood in the comedic waters and could not help herself. "Oh, Ellen, no! We're Jews. We don't believe in tragedy. We believe in horror, atrocity, and injustice, and we recognize them all as inherently hilarious."

At that Grandpa and Paul both laughed, and Ellen raised her hands in surrender. If it was to be a battle of jokes, she knew she could not compete.

To emphasize the urgency of her statement, Grandma leaned across the table directly toward Daniel and poked at the side of his head with a stiff finger. "Never forget."

Daniel hadn't. He had remembered every moment of the conversation and, over the years, he had understood with increasing wonder just what his grandparents were so funny about. As he learned their history, and the larger history of which they had been a part, the series of jokes came into focus one at a time until he realized that the miracle of his grandparents was not their mere survival— it was their ability to remember and still to feel joy. The miracle was that their laughter was genuine and warm, not manic.

On the sidewalk outside the club, he recounted the important information to his father. "Grandma said, 'We're Jews. We don't believe in tragedy.'"

Paul snorted, and smoke came with it. "She also said,

'Never forget.' Look where that got her."

Daniel chuckled. "That's funny."

"Don't use it."

"Only if you promise that you will."

"What? You mean in conversations?"

"Maybe you can sneak into an academic treatise on the danger of cliché. Or when you're talking to your therapist about how insensitive and inappropriate your son is."

Paul shook his head. He stamped his feet in the cold as though it could warm him up. He pulled on the cigarette as though <u>that</u> could warm him up.

"Do you remember the night she said that to me? Thanksgiving? '74?"

"Said what to you?"

"That we don't believe in tragedy. She and Grandpa were doing shtick together. You and Mom were very upset."

"I think I've blocked most of those Thanksgivings out. They were . . . difficult for me."

"That's why I have to wrap it all in jokes, Dad. All the horror. All the loss. All the injustice. It's the only way to preserve it. Without the lens it hurts too much. It gets blocked. That's what they were telling me. That's why they were so, so funny together. You don't remember that conversation?"

Paul shook his head. He shrugged. Those holidays had been problematic. Tension beforehand raising dread. Ellen's parents always judging him for his lack of financial savvy, poking at him for the years he had spent barely supporting her and the kids before he got his footing. The overcooked, overly ostentatious meals that served as a passive aggressive demonstration of decadent opulence.

The dirty jokes that were supposed to seem risqué and naughty rather than vulgar just because they came from people with grey hair, not from construction workers.

"You muttered and cursed about how inappropriate they were all the way home in the station wagon." Daniel chuckled. "It was pretty hilarious."

Paul shrugged, unable to find the humor. "I don't remember."

LAYOVER (THREE)

Lindsay sucked overpriced orange juice through a plastic straw and watched her father collect his glass of amber liquid and leave cash on the bar. He returned with the gait of a man who refused to acknowledge an injury.

"Did anyone try to steal my bag?"

"A small band of ninjas. I took care of it."

"Well done." He settled onto the tall stool and turned the ice in his drink with his stir straw. He tapped it at the edge of his glass and then placed it carefully on a cocktail napkin. "Okay. This is good. You're doing okay. Yeah?"

"Yeah. I'm fine."

"Great! Well. It was good seeing you."

She had heard the bit before. She smiled politely but could not muster an actual laugh. He had a long layover and she had managed to beg off the last time, let Danny take the weight for her. Today Danny was in Albuquerque and she felt more uncomfortable making her father kill two and a half hours alone at an airport than she felt sitting with him for at least some of that time.

"I can't believe Daniel can afford to come down here every time you have a layover."

"I don't understand."

"It winds up being pretty expensive. I mean, not just the eight-dollar orange juice—"

"He always has coffee."

"Of course. And there's gas, and the parking down here is exorbitant."

"He's never complained."

"Right. He wouldn't."

"Do you need me to cover your parking?"

"Me? No. Are you kidding?"

Paul studied her, trying to see through to the meaning behind the words. He could usually do that with people, but Lindsay had always been an irritating mystery to him. An enigma wrapped in incomprehensible resentment.

"But I think Daniel's always about a quarter to broke."

"I don't think it's been as bad since he quit smoking pot." Paul watched his daughter to see whether anything in her expression would tell him that Daniel had lied about that. He couldn't tell anything.

"Still. I worry about him. There's no union, you know?"

"What?"

"For comedians. There's no union. No 401k. No insurance. No . . . safety net."

"He hasn't come to us for anything in a while."

"When was he coming to you for anything?"

"Oh." He let that drop. "He's grown into a pretty terrific comic."

"Comedian."

"There's a difference?"

"Instead of a graphic tee shirt under a flannel button-down he wears a jacket and tie."

Paul chuckled.

"Also, he quit smoking pot."

"Right." Paul sipped his scotch. "I watched a few episodes of your show."

Lindsay said nothing. She waited.

"There's some really good dialogue in there."

Lindsay nodded. The words felt loaded. They felt carefully chosen. They seemed to deliberately leave out so much else about the show even as they took the shape of a compliment.

"You're working with the tension between the words in a way I've never seen anyone do it in television."

"Did you ever see *The Wire*?"

"No. I don't—I think you know I don't really watch much TV."

"I do. I do know that." She had set her phone to sound an alarm at the forty-five-minute mark so that she could make a graceful exit, claiming urgency if things were too difficult. She knew it could not possibly be nearing that time yet. She doubted it had been ten minutes. "Which ones did you watch?"

"The first three. I figured I'll do them in order."

"Oh, good! You're going to keep on?"

"Oh, yeah. I'm very interested to see where it goes."

"That's really nice to hear."

"It's kind of unnerving when you put my subtext on the screen."

Lindsay leaned in, now. "Now *I'm* interested to see where it goes."

"What do you mean?"

"Where are you recognizing your subtext on the screen?"

Paul drank. "I noticed it right off in the first episode. When they leave the grandparents' house. The whole family in their ridiculous coats and scarves and there's all that business of saying goodbye at the door and him refusing to take tupperwares full of leftovers and they bundle into the car and take off all the outerwear in silence as the car warms up and then they pull out of the driveway and the first thing the guy says—"

"Lawrence."

"Right. The first thing Lawrence says is, 'Well. That was relatively painless.' I laughed aloud when I heard that. It was always what was going on in my head at those sorts of things."

"You're kidding, right?"

"What do you mean?"

"That wasn't subtext, Dad. You always said that aloud."

"I did?"

"Every time. Mom's parents. Your parents. Your brother's place in Manhattan. Every time. We'd get in the car and if Daniel or I started to talk you'd put up a finger and say, 'three-minute rule,' to keep us from saying whatever you imagined we were going to say within any possible earshot of the relatives. The indication that we were far enough out of range was when you said, 'Well, that was relatively painless.' Then we could start to talk."

Paul turned his glass on the cocktail napkin and the napkin turned with it. "Huh. I don't remember that."

Lindsay sipped her orange juice. She realized she was rationing herself. She didn't want to finish it, didn't want this to be a two-beverage conversation.

"Well then, you certainly captured the moment."

Lindsay nodded. "If you keep watching—"

"I will. I'm going to."

Lindsay went on as though he hadn't interrupted, "—You'll see a bunch of stuff that feels like us."

Paul paused for a moment, went through a little performance of choosing not to say something, and then deciding to say it. "And Lawrence is gay. Yeah?"

"Yeah."

"But Noreen doesn't know."

"She has suspicions. That starts to come out before the end of the first season."

Paul nodded slowly.

"Do you want to have this conversation? I mean . . . Are we going to have this conversation?"

"Your mother knows who I am."

"Okay."

"She doesn't like to think about it. She doesn't like to talk about it."

"I'm right though. Yeah?"

"I don't know."

Lindsay waited. She sipped her orange juice. She knew her father well enough to know that he wouldn't let that kind of a lie stand. She was right.

"I think of myself as bisexual."

She waited.

"It's not like I can't perform with a woman. You know. With your mother."

"Well, that certainly sounds like a life of impulsive passion."

Paul barked an uncharacteristic laugh. She had expected a subdued snort, but the sharp sound made her laugh in response. "I'm going to need another drink."

"You haven't finished that one yet."

"I didn't mean I was empty. I meant this is going to be at least a two-scotch talk." He sipped then set his glass down on the napkin. He dipped his straw into the scotch, put a fingertip over the end of the straw to catch a bit of liquid in the suction and then used the straw to draw a careful line of alcohol around the bottom of the glass. When he turned his drink again it tore out a near-perfect circle of paper that stuck to the bottom of the glass when he lifted it to sip. "Yeah. You're probably right."

"But you stay." Lindsay did her best to sound concerned, interested in her father and his decisions, but she knew even as she said it that whatever his response was would shape the direction of her next six episodes. She knew that she was doing professional research as much as she was seeing her father as vulnerable and honest as he had ever been with her. She suddenly understood why Daniel kept meeting him at the airport for his layovers. She understood why it left her brother introspective and ever-so-slightly changed each time.

"I'm certainly not at one of the far ends of the sexual spectrum." He finished the drink in a long pull and then said, "In all of your thinking and writing and exploration of my sexuality, Kid, I think you've failed to notice the most important factor."

Lindsay searched his eyes at the same time she searched her own memories, her own experiences for the thing he was hinting at.

Paul leaned forward and spoke softly, as though what he was saying was a secret. He brought his face so close to hers that she could smell the alcohol on his breath and behind it, the tobacco. "I love her." Then he made the movement into the weight shift that led to him standing up from the awkwardly high seat. He captured his glass in his left hand and said, "You want another orange juice? Is that just plain orange juice?"

"Not yet. I'm still doing okay on this one."

Paul headed up to the bar.

Lindsay thought about the implications of what he had just said. She thought about how her character's entire arc could be changed if the gravity that drew him to the difficult relationship she had established for him was not indebtedness or shame, not guilt or fear, but simple love.

She tore a strip from one edge of her napkin.

She thought about how much darker, how much sadder that would make the betrayal his impulses had led him to. She thought about how many times in scenes with the wife, he hadn't said that he loved her and how few times she had ever heard her father say it to her mother. Even telling Lindsay that he loved his wife, he had delivered it like a dangerous and powerful secret.

She thought about how pathetic her desire was to hear her father profess his love for her, to hear him say that he was proud of her, to hear him say, clearly and simply, that he had liked the show. She sipped her orange juice.

She tore the last width of her napkin into two long strips and added them to the small collection of strips that she didn't fully remember creating.

Paul rejoined her, scotch in hand. "I had her make it a double. It's a long layover."

"Has Mom got her drinking under control at all?"

"She's not the one you have to worry about." He raised his glass at her.

"You've always been functional and self-aware about

it."

Paul shrugged. "She tries to keep it to two a night."

"Tries?"

Paul closed his eyes and pushed his head forward while he patted the air with his hands, a gesture she knew well, a gesture that meant, 'just let this lie. It's more of a battle than I want to take on.'

They sipped in companionable silence for a while.

"Do you know there's a company that comes up at the end of each of your shows called Family Dynamic?"

Lindsay snorted. "Yes. Yes, I do."

"Sorry. I don't really know how it works? Is that who you work for?"

"That's my company. We own the show."

"I thought it was TNT."

"TNT is the initial broadcaster but there are a lot of different producing entities that work with any network, especially in cable. They've got first rights, but I can still take it elsewhere for syndication if it lasts long enough to have a full package. Or, you know, there's other options now. Netflix. Amazon. Also, there's some potential for European release."

"Nothing works the way it used to."

"That's correct."

"Things were very different when your mother and I met. When we got married."

Lindsay wanted to know where he was going. She wanted to let him speak. She carefully wove the strips of her cocktail napkin into a mesh as if she was a child working on a kindergarten crafts project.

"People have a lot more options now."

Lindsay pulled the last of her orange juice through the

straw with a slurping sound. She waved at the bartender and signaled that her glass was empty. He nodded.

"So . . . does it look like that'll happen?"

"Like what will happen?" Her phone made a chirping noise. She reached into her purse and pushed a button to silence it.

"Do you have to get that?"

"No. That's not a sound of urgency."

Paul nodded. "*The Full Monty* thing."

"What?"

"For syndication."

"Oh! Package. A full syndication package."

"Right. Sorry. I don't know the language."

"That's okay."

"Your mother keeps thinking the show is on something called The Dynamite Network."

"I know."

"I haven't corrected her. I don't think she'd enjoy the show." He paused and then he said, "I think there are aspects of it that would upset her."

Lindsay felt a combination of sadness and rage which she expressed by ignoring them entirely. "That generally requires a hundred episodes and I'm starting to think we'll get there. There's been some talk about a two-season commitment coming in, and if that happens, we're golden. We're coming into the end of our third season now and we're still getting pretty good ratings."

"Well that sounds terrific."

"We've got a really loyal fan base. Every week, three or four members of the cast live tweet the show and there are hashtag games that go on and audience involvement."

"Jesus. I feel like I'm listening to dialogue from an

abstruse science fiction film."

"There are no science fiction films anymore. Just movies."

Paul pulled his head backward as though someone had flicked at his nose. He said, "What's that distinction about?"

Lindsay said, "Films wear jackets and ties and don't smoke pot."

Paul laughed. "Nice."

"It's a callback. Learned it from Daniel." The bartender brought Lindsay her orange juice.

"He's okay though, right?"

"Who?"

"Daniel."

"Yeah. He's okay."

"The last time I saw him it looked like he had put on some weight."

"Are you kidding me?"

"Not bad, you know. He wasn't obese. But he looked soft."

Lindsay sipped her orange juice. "Yeah. He's okay."

"What happened there? Your jaw got very tense."

"Daniel is fine. His weight is fine."

"Well, I wasn't saying it wasn't fine. It's just that I know sometimes weight gain can be a symptom of something else. You know. Depression. What-have-you."

"He's fine. He's booking gigs. He's being hilarious."

"I saw him in New York."

"I know. You took the train down from Boston."

"I took the train down from Boston. He was funny."

"He always is."

"There was one bit I think he has to stop doing."

"I know. He wrote a long piece about how his father said he should stop doing the bit."

Paul squeezed his nose for a moment, taking that in. "I was thinking of asking you not to keep putting my sexuality in your show."

"It's a character, Dad. It's not you."

"You know what I mean."

"I think you're going to like where it's all going."

Paul nodded slowly, realizing that she was not going to change the show to protect him. "I'll keep watching."

"Okay. I'll keep writing and producing."

"You do that. You seem to be pretty good at it." He sipped his drink and Lindsay could see that his focus had begun to soften. His gestures were becoming a little bit more vague and a little bit more broad simultaneously.

She sipped her orange juice and watched him from an uncomfortable position of judgment and with a degree of pity, though she could not quite admit that to herself, could not name the feeling.

Paul saw her look and entirely misinterpreted it. "I'm not saying that he's fat. Not like when you gained all that weight after Michelle died."

"She didn't die. She committed suicide."

Paul raised his shoulders and closed his eyes, conceding the point.

"And I wasn't fat."

"Oh, don't do that, Honey."

"What am I doing?"

"You were fat."

"I was a little bit overweight."

"We have pictures. You were . . . Never mind. It doesn't matter."

Lindsay watched as her father destroyed a second cocktail napkin, this time creating a rougher, less satisfying paper disc. She said, "Here," and slid her torn and reconstructed napkin over to him.

"You made me a kindergarten potholder. I'm touched." He flattened it, smoothing the weave lovingly and then set his drink on it.

"After Michelle killed herself, I gained nine pounds."

Paul nodded. "And now you're dating Tessa."

"I live with Monique."

"Right. Monique. Who's Tessa?"

"Tessa is my assistant."

"Right. Your assistant."

"Yes."

"Because you need an assistant to run your company where you make television shows that you own and license to giant corporations."

"Yes."

Paul took a deep breath. "I really am sorry, you know."

"Okay," Lindsay had no idea what he was sorry about.

Paul made a gesture, broad and vague that she thought meant, 'all of it. Everything.' What he said was, "We both really liked Michelle. She shouldn't have done that. I know it was . . . hard for you."

She said, "Okay," but what she meant was, 'it would have been nice to hear that at the time.' Then she added, "I don't think it's for us to say what she should or shouldn't have done."

Paul nodded. "Someday I'll tell you about Michael Donelly."

"I don't know who that is."

"That's because I haven't told you about him yet."

Lindsay nodded. "Did he commit suicide?"

"He tried. Hurt himself very badly." After a brief pause he repeated, "Very badly," and ran a finger down his cheek as if that indicated a particularly bad kind of injury, though Lindsay did not know what the gesture was meant to indicate.

"And he was . . ." She left a long gap, hoping Paul would fill it in, but he didn't so she guessed, ". . . a friend?"

"He didn't want me to marry your mother."

Lindsay took that in. She let the pieces fit together in her head, the implied back story, the implied confession of something undefined but fully realized behind the inebriated clues.

She said, "At Michelle's funeral, I met her mother. I sat with her and she looked straight ahead. I remembered Michelle telling me that one of things she liked about us—"

"About who?"

"Us. You. Me. Mom. Daniel. Us."

"I didn't know she liked us."

"She said she liked the way we look at each other. Not just when we talk, or whatever. She said we all do it. She said we watch one another like we're trying to spot poker tells."

Paul snorted and squeezed his nose.

Her phone made a sound that was not an alarm she had set. She wanted not to have heard it. She wanted to stay with this conversation, with this iteration of her father, balanced on a three-legged stool of alcohol, intimacy, and reminiscence.

"Is that a sound of urgency?"

She offered a sad nod.

"I know. It's a workday for you. Go ahead."

She found the phone in her bag. She moved her thumb about on the screen, selecting the app, opening the text. She read it. She read it again. She put the phone away.

"Bad news?" Her father asked.

She shook her head. "Very good news." There was no way she could explain to him how good the news was. He could not possibly understand the significance, not just financially for her, but in terms of her career, her status in a male-dominated industry, the actual power that had just fallen to her as a byproduct of the success she had just achieved.

"Is it about *Served Cold*?"

"We're picked up for two more seasons. Forty-four more episodes."

"Well that's terrific. I suppose that's the sort of thing people in Hollywood would congratulate you for. I'm sure everyone at your company is very proud."

He had come so close and he had been so open, so vulnerable moments earlier that she took a chance before she had time to control the impulse, before she knew what she was risking. "Dad, do you like the show? Are you proud of the work I'm doing?"

Paul said, and he said it with absolute sincerity, "Honey, you have good ratings and loyal fans with cast tweets and hashtags and now you have a full syndication package. I don't know what you think you need my approval for."

"I should probably . . . "

"Yeah. That sounds like something you should stay on top of."

Lindsay stood up to go.

"Seriously, if you need me to cover your parking . . ."

"No. I'm good. I've got it."

She hugged him, and he hugged her without standing up from the stool. She wondered how many more drinks he would have alone in the airport in the time he had left there.

She put money on the bar for her orange juice, hoisted her carry-all purse onto her shoulder and left the bar, but she circled back past the partition that separated the seating area from the walkway and said to her father, "You fly safely, would you?"

Paul said, "Oh! I don't think they're going to put me in charge!"

They both chuckled and she walked away. She turned back and knew, in an embarrassed sort of way, that she was looking to see whether he was watching her go.

He was not watching her go.

Unaware of her gaze, he folded the woven napkin carefully into his pocket and turned his glass on the unprotected tabletop, allowing it to weep a ring print of condensation right there on the exposed surface.

TWO EMAILS

FROM: DGrunman@gmail.com
TO: Louis Markham <louis.Markham@fastnet.net>
Subject: Affection, Avoidance, and About Damn Time

Dear Louis,

Firstly, let me say that I miss you a great deal. I think of you often, wonder how you're doing, and then get on with my life, wholly failing to reach out in any way at all. I get your annual Holiday letters with the photos of you and Joanne and the kid who looks more like an actual person with each passing year and then . . . another year passes and I'm still a reclusive lout who hasn't bothered to touch base and say, "Hey! Howzitall going?"

Hey! Howzitall going?

Secondly, let me confess that as much as I owe you this note, it serves an ulterior purpose that I willingly confess, making it—you know—just another purpose and not so ulterior at all. (It occurs to me that there's a joke to be written about Sir Mix-a-Lot having Posterior Motives, but I'll figure out how to phrase it later. Because obviously the world needs more joke based on vulgar songs from the early nineties.) I am writing this e-mail partly as an avoidance, an evasion, a productive procrastination.

I should be sending my mother an e-mail. No. I should be calling her but decided instead to send an e-mail. I don't want to write that e-mail almost as much as I don't want to talk on the phone with her, though, so I'm writing to you instead. Also, I did the dishes and tidied my desk. And took a bag of trash out for pick-up. Burned copies of a bunch of Butch Walker CDs for Lindsay who doesn't know who he is 'cause I think she should start using his music on her show. (You know that Lindsay created *Served Cold,* right? Now she's doing a new show called *Day Drinking with Doris* on Netflix that's loosely based on her relationship with Mom and, I suspect, closely based on mine).

So, Mom left me a voicemail that Dad is dead. I saw that it was Mom calling and I pushed it to voicemail 'cause I'm an asshole and then the voicemail said that Dad had died, and I felt terrible. She rambled a bunch, but what it came down to is that he died last night napping on the couch, and she didn't realize it and figured she'd let him sleep through until he woke up and came to join her but in the morning he hadn't moved and she realized he was gone. So, she started making phone calls and one of them was to me and I pushed it to voicemail. She meandered through a bunch of logistics and could I be home for the get-together/memorial thing tomorrow.

So, Dad is dead. And I got a ticket for the red eye tonight. And Mom called and I pushed her to voicemail and now I'm avoiding writing her an email 'cause it seems like there's so much to say that it can't possibly fit into words. You know? Once, when we were tripping on a Saturday in the Silverthorne building after you showed me how to open the deadbolt with a butter knife, you said you felt like you were talking through the wrong end of the binoculars. It feels a little bit like that only with a lot more complicated facets. It's like writing through the wrong end of a kaleidoscope.

Do you remember when we had a long conversation about how when we wrote letters home from school, we were always trying to find enough things to say in the letters so that the inevitable request for money didn't feel like the point of the letter? We were getting stoned out on the big rock on the far side of the lacrosse field and the mist had filled in around us so that we couldn't even see the little path where the security truck went by every half hour or something. When the truck came, we'd see the headlights round the curve by Gould Hall and we'd go silent and lie down on the rock even though there was no possible way anyone would see us if we were dancing out there in pink boas in the fog. But when the headlights came, we'd lie down on the cold rock and giggle, passing the joint back and forth awkwardly. It felt like a great act of courage to be outside smoking a joint instead of huddled in our room, doing bong hits and blowing the smoke into a rolled-up towel.

I think for me, prep school was largely an extended *Hogan's Heroes* Live Action Role Play. The security truck headlights were the cold, bright searchlights of the watch towers, the faculty and dorm staff the lovable, incompetent Klinks and Schultzes. We were young and good looking, brave and secretive, sneaking out to break the rules, getting back before anyone knew we'd been gone.

In any case, while we were talking about how we were always trying to mask the real reason for our letters home I had a thought that I didn't say aloud because I thought it would make me less cool and, besides, we were riffing fast and funny on the clever ways of slipping in the request for cash and I didn't want to lose that thread. God, I loved bantering with you. You were the first person I ever met who could throw down wit at the same pace as me. Whenever you and I got on a tear, building one joke onto another, playing casually competitive Top-that-Line, I felt as though I might not be entirely alone in the world.

The only other person who ever came close to understanding those rhythms was my dad and even he didn't play out a thread the way you could with me. He mostly just got one volley and then graded my humor. "You can use that!" or, "I don't think there's anything there."

The thing I didn't say that night because I was too busy being funny and getting high was that sometimes it felt to me as though I was only writing to ask for money as an excuse to make contact without admitting that I still needed contact with my parents. The thing we were discussing, disguising in our letters was also in its own way a disguise. Maybe that was just me.

My family has a lot of weirdness around money. Around money, around gifts, about how and when we help and how and when we don't help one another. It often felt as though giving me money was the only way my Mom knew how to show her love and asking for money was the only way I knew how to show mine and then the money would become a point of resentment at both ends of the exchange, so the love got all hostile and tense.

I'm getting philosophical in my middle age. I've been writing essays instead of just jokes and bits and spec scripts to try to get television work lately. Something happened after I quit smoking pot. For a while I was afraid I would never be able to write anything again. Then I wrote a bunch of really angry stuff. Then I started writing these essays and they delve into stuff that's really uncomfortable. Some of them are funny. I don't know if you read my stuff online when it shows up or if you follow me on social media and stuff, but the writing had gotten so much better. I used to think I had to be stoned to be creative and I didn't realize that the pot was keeping me locked into a mindset I'd developed in my teens. I was just stuck on a rock, hiding in a fog all those years.

Then I stopped smoking pot and I slowly realized that I was learning new things, finding new directions in my work that I didn't even know I craved until I started feeling again. I always thought I was going to die young. I don't know if you'll remember that. I thought I was going to die when I was twenty-seven. Then, when I passed my twenty-eighth birthday, I figured it'd be thirty-seven. I had this dream of immortality that can only really be achieved with unfulfilled potential and then . . . I quit smoking pot and I outlived my anticipated expiration date and I discovered I wanted to achieve my full potential. If I'm gonna live, I guess, I figured I might as well put something I could be really proud of into the world.

When I was a kid, my father told me once that the mark of a great artist is the ability to make it look effortless and I was too young to really understand that, so I went around thinking that I couldn't be good at anything if it didn't come easy. I spent all that time doing stand-up and writing spec scripts and staying high the whole time just to make it as clear as I possibly could that I wasn't putting in any effort at all. Now I'm working my ass off all the time, trying to write cleaner, to dig deeper, to take more risk and people keep telling me it doesn't seem fair to them that it comes so easy to me.

I try to explain that it's not easy; it's just necessary. Or I glibly blow it off, saying that I have to be incredibly productive to compensate for a lack of talent or marketable skills. None of that is really it, though. I used to plan to die young and that freed me to be all play all the time. Now I know how much time there really is in a life and I'm laboring under the crushing urgency of mortality.

Huh. I wrote that sentence, that phrase, "the crushing urgency of mortality," and I thought, *oooh. I should call my Dad. He'd like that.* I wonder how long I can expect those moments to keep happening.

It happened once after Garry Shandling died. I wrote a joke I thought he would like, and I was reaching for the phone before I realized he wouldn't answer. It was the most Shandling joke I ever wrote. *About a year ago I accidentally said, "my Mom," when I meant, "My Girlfriend" and it freaked me out so badly that for about a month I couldn't have sex with either of them.*

I should have called you. You would have laughed at that. And given me a tag.

Sometimes my best tags and callbacks are written by the introjection of you that I carry with me, the one I banter with internally when I'm in the car on a long drive. I had a joke I'd been doing for a while, *I've been in this relationship long enough that I suggest sex and she tells me what time it is.* I'd been doing it for—I don't know—a year and a half or something and one night on the way to a gig I was running the set in my head and when I did that joke, you blurted out a tag in my mind and I laughed aloud. If I hadn't been driving I might've high-fived imaginary you. So now I tag it with, *Last month she bought me an engraved watch. It said, "Now can we stop having this conversation?"*

Every time I do it, I feel like you wrote that joke for me, like it's you getting the laugh.

So now my Dad is dead, and my Mom is alone, and I avoided her call and I'm writing an email to you to avoid writing an email to her that gets more difficult to write the less I write it.

Do you ever get to Los Angeles? I can't imagine having much of an excuse to come to Ohio, but man, I would love to see you again.

Could you tell Joanne I'm sorry I hit on her when you guys first started going out? I still feel like an asshole about that. It's one of those things that, if I think about it while I'm shaving, I cut myself a little bit with the razor. Not like a teenage girl who cuts herself. I mean, the thought of that evening just makes me wince and twitch and the next thing you know I've got a bloody dot of toilet paper that I'm trying to remember to clean off before I go to some meeting or something that I've had to shave for.

I think back over all those meetings, all those pitches that went badly or went well but still went nowhere. I think about the drives to and from, about the scripts and the cold calls and the disappointments and I know how much better it would all have been if you'd been out here, if I'd just had the balls all those years ago to say, "Damn, you're funny. Let's be partners. Let's work on this stuff together," instead of yelling at you and telling you your thoughts on my script were stupid. I know I was insulting and cruel. I didn't know how to be wrong for so, so long. So, I got mad and I shut you out instead of thanking you and making the script better and maybe getting something sold.

Blowing up that conversation was probably the first in a long series of self-sabotaging acts of vast stupidity.

Crap. Okay. My playlist has just circled around to *Going Back / Going Home* for the second time (Third? I know it's not the first time I've heard it during this email). I should wrap this up and write the one to my Mom.

If you ever want to talk, I promise not to send you to voicemail if I see your number on the caller I.D.

I miss you more than you might imagine all the time, and more than that today.

xoxoxo ox (affection and an ox),

Daniel

———

FROM: DGrunman@gmail.com

TO: Mom <EllenGrun@SusquehannaTimeCode.Net>

Dear Mom,

I'm so sorry you're having to deal with all these logistics on your own. I'll be on the red-eye out of LAX. United 726.

Love,

Daniel

TRANSPARENCY

"Hi, Mom." Daniel stood up to hug her as she approached. His knee bumped the corner of the table as he moved, and his coffee sloshed out of the cup into the china saucer. A waiter appeared at once to take it away.

"I was just coming by to warm this up for you anyway, Mr. Grunman," the waiter said. "I'll just bring you a fresh one."

"This place is so fancy. You remember you used to come into town and you would come to the apartment and I would feed you?"

"I do remember that." He remembered the endlessly repeated list of his favorite childhood foods, each item accompanied by commentary. *Those bologna sandwiches,* she would say, *with the mustard. I always preferred mayonnaise, but you had to have mustard on yours or you just wouldn't eat them. You remember?* And he would say, *I remember.* Then, after a pause, *And peanut butter and jelly. You used to put potato chips right on the sandwich. No matter how many times I explained to you that the potato chips go separately, you would open up the sandwich and put them right inside. You remember?* And he would say, *I remember.*

At a certain point he had lost the ability to be certain of what he actually remembered and what he remembered only as part of their call-and-response ritual. "Thanks for coming uptown to meet me. My timing on this trip is . . . very tight."

"Oh, Honey. I don't mind coming uptown. Not to meet you. I just took the E up to 14th and then the shuttle over for the 6. Easy-peasy, really."

"I had hoped I could get a real break in the day to come down closer to you. Save you the trouble. Somewhere walking distance."

"No real trouble, Honey. Truly. I don't really walk as much as I used to. It's not my legs. My legs can take it. It's just, I run out of breath. Isn't that something? I used to be in such good shape. Now—"

"But I really did want to get a chance to see you while I was here." That part was entirely for her benefit. He had tried to schedule the trip so tightly that he would have no time at all to spare. When that proved impossible, he had hoped against likelihood that she would be unwilling or unable to travel all the way up to the East Side to visit with him.

As though he had not spoken, she went on, seated now, taking off her gloves and carefully stacking them beside her silverware. "—I can hardly go a block before I'm reaching for my inhaler. Did I tell you I have an inhaler now? It's the stuff they give to people with asthma. But I don't have asthma. Not really. Do you mind if I smoke?"

"I don't think you're allowed to in here."

"I suppose not. They don't let you smoke anywhere anymore. It's a subtle kind of fascism."

"Yes. That's the problem with fascism. The health regulations."

"Very funny. Anyway, I don't walk so much anymore. I just took a cab over to the E train and then the E to 14th."

"Yes. And then the shuttle." He heard the dismissive snark in his voice, and wished he could take it back, but that moment was gone, and she hadn't noticed the tone.

"Right. And then the 6. And the cab from the train to here was literally just six dollars."

"I can reimburse you. I'm sorry it was such a hassle."

"Not a hassle at all. You worry too much. And, as I said, literally six dollars. Including the un-fare. That's what I call the money that's on the meter before you even tell them where you want to go. I call that the un-fare."

"That's funny."

"You can use it if you like."

"I probably won't."

"In one of your little stories or whatever."

"Okay." He opened the menu and looked at it for a bit. "Are you eating?"

"I'm not sure. I'm not really hungry."

"I don't mean right now, silly." She patted his hand. "I mean, in general."

"Oh. Yes. Yes, I am."

The waiter set down his fresh coffee for him along with a new tin tank of half-and-half.

"Do you have Jameson?" Ellen asked the waiter.

"I beg your pardon?"

"Jameson? Irish whiskey? Most people say 'Jameson's' with the possessive, but it's actually just called Jameson."

"Ah. No, ma'am. I'm sorry. We don't have a full bar."

"Dewar's then."

"We only serve wine and beer, ma'am."

"Oh," Ellen's disappointment was palpable.

"Sorry," Daniel said. "I didn't know."

"Oh, that's all right, Honey." Then she said to the waiter, "Could I just have the cheese and bacon panini? Extra crispy for the bacon?"

"Of course. I love those." The waiter said. "And, anything to drink?"

"Just . . . I don't know. Just iced tea, I guess."

"All right. And for you sir?"

"Just keep refilling my coffee until I vibrate and die. Thanks."

The waiter chuckled politely, took the menus and went away.

"Lindsay does that too. All the time. The wait staff at restaurants. Door men. Always making jokes with the people."

"You get to see her often?"

"Every few weeks, since she's been in town. She's very busy."

"She's running a show." He stirred in the cream, tapped the spoon, set it aside, lining it up with the edge of a small cocktail napkin.

"I thought you said you were eating."

"In general. Not right now."

"Anyway . . ." She gestured as though she was about to go on, paused for a long moment, and at last asked, "What was I saying?"

He considered, 'you were beginning the fishing expedition. You asked if I was eating as a way of leading up to questions about my finances, about my work, about my life.' He said, "I don't remember. Something about the price of cabs."

"Huh. I don't recall now. It can't have been important."

"No. I suppose not."

"If I pay for lunch will you have something?"

"No. I'm paying for lunch and either way I won't be having anything."

"Except coffee."

"That's right." He sipped his coffee.

The waiter brought her iced tea and she sipped it. Her lips turned downward in disapproval of the taste.

"This is how I know I'm not an alcoholic," she announced, unprompted. "If I go out and they don't have what I want to drink, mostly Scotch or Irish, I'll just have something else. I don't really like wine or beer. So, I just won't drink for now."

"Good for you."

"You don't drink at all, do you?"

"Occasionally. I'm trying to remain fully present as much as possible."

"But, occasionally?"

"Mostly if it's a business thing and I don't want the other person to feel like they're being judged."

"That's funny."

"Is it?"

"Yes. You really do come up with some very witty things sometimes."

"Thank you."

"Anyway, I've always been very careful not to let myself become an addict. Your father and I, when we used to travel, sometimes we would go out somewhere for dinner or to a show or something and they wouldn't have scotch there, or Irish. Sometimes he would drink wine, but

I never much liked wine. So, I could just wait until we got back to our hotel, or we could stop at a bar later, on our way or whatever. It was never that important to me."

"Yes. I can see that."

She sipped her iced tea again, her lips presenting a broad indication of distaste. He saw the tiny creases around her lips, cultivated over years of pulling smoke through filters and broadly indicating distaste at spiritless beverages and sentimentality in the arts. "So, is that what you're in town about?"

The question took him by surprise. He tried to catch up, failed. He said, "Your mathematical proofs that you are not an alcoholic?"

"No, you goofball!" She patted his hand affectionately. "You know. Your writing. We were just talking about it."

"We were?"

"A little. You said something funny. I commented on it. You know."

"Ah. Yes. Yes. That's what I'm in town about."

"Good news, I hope."

He shrugged noncommittally. "I won't really know until after the meetings."

"You used to tell me everything. You remember that?"

He nodded. He did remember. "I have to be careful now."

"Oh, come on! It's not as though I'm going to steal your ideas."

He snorted. "That's not what I mean."

The waiter refilled his coffee and said, "Your sandwich should be ready in just a minute."

"Sometimes . . . I just have to keep my work separate from you."

"I don't know what that means. What could happen?"

He sipped his coffee and decided to try speaking some subtext aloud. "I used to feel you were living through my accomplishments."

"Now you feel I'm living through your inheritance," she said.

He chuckled. "That's very funny."

"You can use it, if you want."

"You know, you can use it."

"Oh, I don't write anymore, Honey. You know that."

"You can if you want."

"Once your father and I got married—"

"I know."

"There was never time after that."

"There's time now."

"I'm going to step outside and smoke while I wait for my sandwich."

"Don't." He felt something important coming, a breakthrough, something to tell his therapist about when he got home.

"Are you sure you don't want a drink?" She asked as though that was connected to anything that had been said thus far.

"No. I'm trying to remain connected to my emotional life as much as possible. It helps a lot with my process."

"Your process?"

"My writing."

"Oh, that's silly. A lot of great writers have been drinkers."

"Yes. I don't think it was the drinking that did it."

She picked up her gloves and gripped them with unnecessary determination. "If you see the waiter could you flag him down? I think I'd like a glass of wine with my sandwich."

"Yes. If I see him."

"Wine isn't my favorite, but it'll do in a pinch."

"I'll flag him down if I see him."

"I think I'm going to step outside for a smoke. As long as the sandwich isn't here yet." She stood up. "Get me something red, but not too sweet."

She walked outside, and he could see her breath even as she tapped a cigarette from the pack. He saw her light it as she had done so many times over the course of his life. She brought the flame toward her face. The light flickered against the tip of her nose. It seemed he could smell the sulfur of the match, the first puff of tobacco smoke. They came with the gesture and rhythm of her motion. There was no parsing fact from fiction, memory from ritual. He muttered, "I remember."

He loved her. He felt the love suddenly, and for just a moment, he thought a glass of wine might be nice.

He decided against. He turned his coffee cup slowly in its saucer. His mother smoked beyond the glass. He watched her. He remained fully present. The window gave him just enough distance. He could love her through the pane.

ABOUT ATMOSPHERE PRESS

Atmosphere Press is an independent, full-service publisher for excellent books in all genres and for all audiences. Learn more about what we do at atmospherepress.com.

We encourage you to check out some of Atmosphere's latest releases, which are available at Amazon.com and via order from your local bookstore:

The Dark Secrets of Barth and Williams College: A Comedy in Two Semesters, a novel by Glen Weissenberger

Stuck and Drunk in Shadyside, a novel by M. Byerly

These Things Happen, a novel by Chris Caldwell

Vanity: Murder in the Name of Sin, a novel by Rhiannon Garrard

Blood of the True Believer, a novel by Brandann R. Hill-Mann

In the Cloakroom of Proper Musings, a lyric narrative by Kristina Moriconi

An Expectation of Plenty, a novel by Thomas Bazar

Sink or Swim, Brooklyn, a novel by Ron Kemper

Lost and Found, a novel by Kevin Gardner

Eaten Alive, a novel by Tim Galati

The Sacrifice Zone, a novel by Roger S. Gottlieb

ABOUT THE AUTHOR

Dylan Brody is an author, award-winning playwright, humorist, filmmaker, executive producer, radio personality, and snappy dresser. He writes, performs, directs, coaches other writers, and facilitates a Weekly Writers' Workshop. As CEO of Active Voice Productions (Liberal Arts Entertainments) he strives to build an ethically sound, foundationally sustainable company to provide

Photo by Cat Gwynn

and elevate entertainment content of the highest artistic quality.

Learn more about him at dylanbrody.com.

Learn more about Active Voice Productions at activevoiceproductions.com.

CPSIA information can be obtained
at www.ICGtesting.com
Printed in the USA
FSHW020626270820
73328FS